Odyssey 2024/2027

Return to the Origin; a Quantum Leap

Leonardo Fibonacci
(Dr. Frog)

Paperback: 978-1-968667-22-1
eBook: 978-1-968667-23-8
Library of Congress Control Number: 2025914113

This is a work of fiction.

Ordering Information:

Prime Seven Media
518 Landmann St.
Tomah City, WI 54660

Printed in the United States of America

"You are unique and different, but no choice." – Ra Uru Hu
"Time is Art, 13:20." – José Argüelles, Valum Votan
"You are dreaming in a dream." – Pacal Votan
*"U-Ching is a Miracle: The New DNA Program, of the
Second Creation. Book of Codes."* – Juryt Abma
"Everything is energy, frequency, and vibration. 3-6-9." – Nikola Tesla
"You are a genius. Walk." – Richard Rudd
"Life is a cosmic joke." – Aristotle's Poetics

What might be considered a prophecy also announces a resounding end, today practically an evidence. Ra Uru Hu experienced an 8-day mystical event where a voice revealed to him how the universe works, how we are designed, and how to confront the great mutation that is pushing us towards an inevitable end. **No choice, you are very lucky!! Jazz, be yourself!!**

Ra states that we have been "trained" to do things and to control, not to see and enjoy. Free yourself from your indoctrinated mind and learn to decide and see—while you still can!

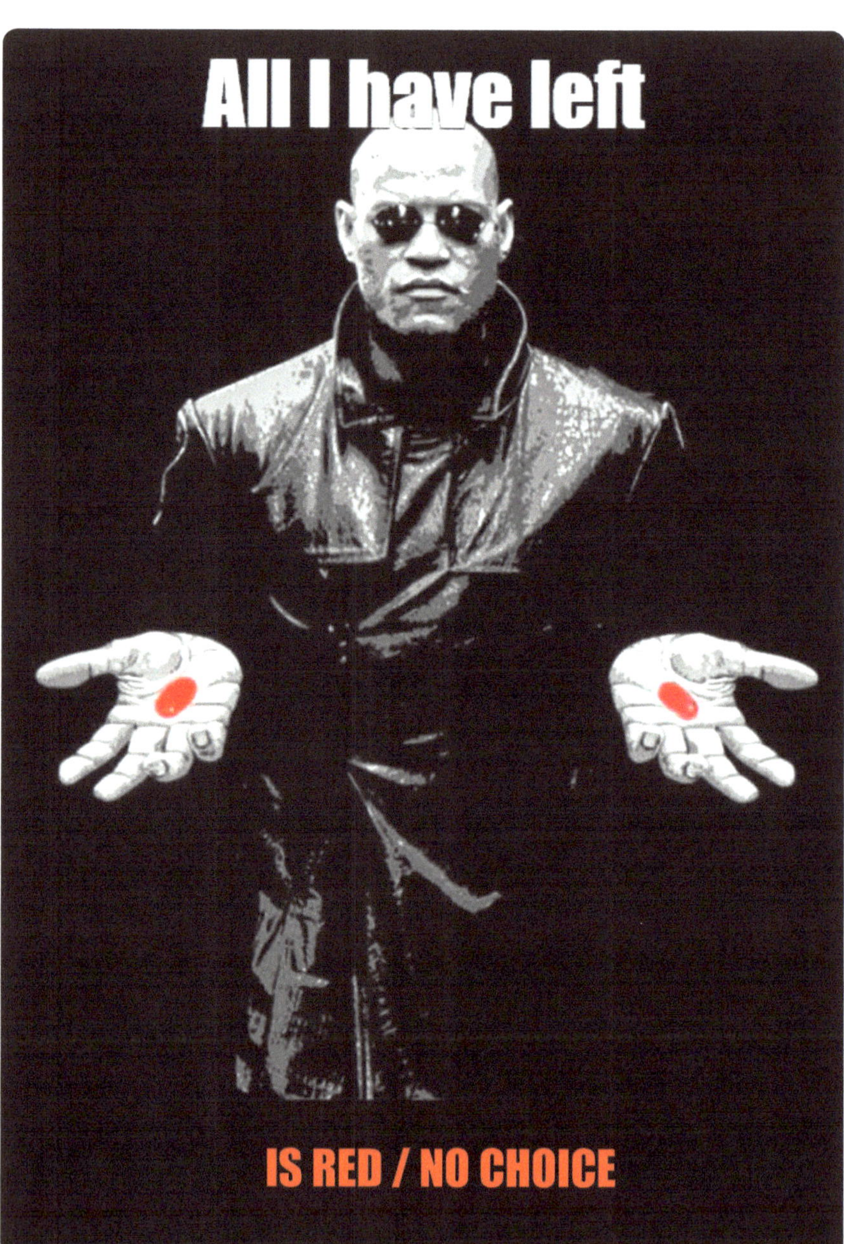
All I have left
IS RED / NO CHOICE

Index

1   Acknowledgements: Om Mani Padme Hum –
The Mantra of Abundance..1

Odissea 2024-2027. Un salt quàntic, retorn l'oriGen.......................3

Prologue 11

2   Prologue: by Juryt Abma 15

3   Nosce te ipsum - Oracle of Delphi: Ad maiorem gloria globi 17

4   Lakshmi, Goddess of Wealth, Royalty, and Freedom.....................23

5   Human Design: The Science of Differentiation 26

6   The Genetic Keys: The Middle Path. Hologenetic Profile,
3 Sequences 35

7   The Tzolkin and the Law of Time 46

8   U-Ching: the new DNA program of the human being;
a book of codes 53

9   In vino veritas: Your truth as a principle of transcendence
and state of consciousness; discover who you truly are.
Oracle of Delphi..60

10 The game of mirrors and the power of endless order:
infinity also exists. 69

11 Between Science and Consciousness 75

12 Hermes Trismegistus: As above, so below.
The Emerald Tablet. 78

13 You have more than you imagine, imagine!! 81

14 It rains manna every day!! 84

15 The bi-verse exists, but you are unique. 87

16 the sweetness of doing nothing 90

17 From nothing, everything is possible, learn to be invisible!! 92

18 The light is indivisible, it's a matter of time: 13:2 94

19 The bio-solar telepathic man, non-egoic – multidimensional 97

20 What does the law of thermodynamics say? 99

21 Delirius Tremens, a Dada delirium: #DadAUal8 102

22 To die and be reborn: To be or not to be 108

23 "Shall we change the world? 111

24 2 Tarot cards and 2 significant characters 113

25 Reflections 117

26 Principles of the Law of Attraction 118

27 The Economy of the Common Good 121

28 Second Part: From Praxis to Paroxysm 123

29 Free energy-free your self 133

30 Personal Reflection on How I Interpret a Calendar Within
Parameters That May Seem Paranormal 143

31 Figs from another basket 150

32 The Bio-Solar Non-Egoic Consciousness and
the Noospheric Man; Dadaist Poem AUal8 170

33 Epilogue 174

1

Acknowledgements: Om Mani Padme Hum – The Mantra of Abundance

This small but significant work, a first opera, is the result of deep research (20 years sounds fast) to address a "journey" that promises to be intense, tumultuous, and fascinating. It is the fruit of readings of all kinds: astrological, mystical, esoteric, philosophical, scientific, and very little of economics.

Here you have a distilled intergalactic voyage, which I hope will also be yours; will you know how to be reborn?

Never before has humanity lived in such a fascinating and tumultuous reality. It may not seem so, but the good news is more than evident; you only need to open your eyes and awaken, for we are in transit—the old world and the new converge and touch! Yes, a new world, absolutely new despite the circumstances and the weight of our own tragedy. Think that the impossible sometimes transcends! Now is the ideal moment to assimilate some transcendental matters and assume that we are self-reflective consciousness, and that abundance is a resonance-frequency with the universe and with oneself at the same time... You must be present and in the right frequency to synchronize or connect with life!

I dedicate this work to my son, Isaac, who indirectly pushed his father to write this. I hope you enjoy it and share it with your loved ones. Son, the night is long but full of stars, and the Sun always rises. I thank my mother, Xel·la, for her patience and support; I hope you understand immortality as a real possibility that you may experience and witness.

I also thank my sister, Pepa, for listening to me and trusting in the love I have for you. I only wish that you also find yourself in this Multiverse that we are co-creating together. Now you are beginning the course of pragmatic philosophy with the change of nodes; I hope you can enjoy this booklet, or Martian guide, which I am sure you will eventually understand and appreciate. Trust in life, even when it hurts.

I do not forget my father, Mariano Pedrol, who always gave me the freedom to live... and to laugh... We love you, wherever you are, we feel you close every day. Rest in peace... This work is also yours, and I dedicate it to you with all the love of a firstborn son, which I have always had for you and will maintain until my last breath!

Introducció: Odissea 2024-2027. Un salt quàntic, retorn l'oriGen.

This book is written in a state of planetary emergency, we are approaching the epicenter of the storm!! Ahead of us are the most intense, complex, and difficult years in modern history. 2027 is imminent, there is nothing to be done, we can only wait… everything has an end, and we cannot resist life itself, but we can position ourselves and also reinvent, we are immersed in a cosmic mutation.

We already know that this "representation," hallucination, or civilization has its days numbered, perhaps it is already a memory/souvenir that no one finds exciting, not even the vast majority of indoctrinated alienated people! We are not aware of it, and I'm not joking, we are witnessing a dramatic, epic, and apocalyptic end!! No choice!!

In fact, we all "know" it, but "we can't understand it," nor do we want to face the reality of it, and we don't take on the responsibility that comes with living through such an intense ending; we can't forget that we will embrace a new era, but we must prepare ourselves, consciously!! We need to deconstruct, reflect, connect, and unlearn, enough with recycled ideas or invented futures like the Metaverse; in my view, we must remain optimistic because we have intelligent, sensitive, and highly valuable information to confront a change that the mind alone cannot easily assimilate, it requires preparation, awareness, and a return to the body—consider yourselves warned!!

A king can issue a decree or do whatever he pleases, but I suspect that none of our kings have lived through a reality so difficult to digest, because we are "programmed with software" that is outdated and needs to be updated carefully in order to restore a modus operandi that is coherent, biohacking!!?? We also know that DNA is mutating to assimilate a transmutation of cosmic order!! The "Catalan intelligence services" have deemed it appropriate to explain and prepare for this Odyssey, here are some basic coordinates for the survival of us, and also of you (each of us must take on a role beyond Catalan identity, because we are and will be, but we need to get ready to enter the New Era). We are all One, but we must take responsibility for our own individuality, reinvent ourselves, and challenge ourselves!! Remember, we are binary consciousness, and love!!

Perhaps what we lack is availability, critical spirit, self-love, and the courage to open Pandora's Box and be reborn!! Will you stay in the 20th century, clinging to an anachronistic modernity based on maintaining a purely materialistic religion that is running out of time?? We must acknowledge that we come from a colonial imperialism that has evolved into a savage capitalism, hostile to life— are we mutating??

We must also recognize that these next six years will affect us deeply because the digital Neocon paradigm continues to feed the beast. They want absolute control over everything that happens… This generates panic, more complexity, and tangible difficulties, so we must stay tuned and awake—everything will be intense and shocking!

The system is obsolete, and many of us are too; perhaps it's time to think about our own transcendence, individually speaking, because civilization and what it represents is losing meaning and charm—let's motivate ourselves. The key is to know how to return to the body and unlearn, to manage real pressure amplified by the mind, which is obsessive and controlling. It's time to address a real, authentic, and sensitive self. We are in transition, and we can no longer think the way we once did. In fact, quantum medicine and cosmic science invite us to reinvent ourselves in order to understand where we are; we must be prepared to enjoy the very miracle of being and seeing. Your rebirth is essential. Decay is absolute, and the collapse will be experienced in real time, because it will be constant and inevitable! As Shakespeare said, *to be or not to be, the rest is silence!*

2027 will be the turning point, from here on out, we will live and see life in an entirely different way—it will be as if our software is being changed, and we must ensure the hardware is in good condition.

Updated!! It will change our mental construct, and we will open ourselves to consciousness in a very particular way, but it won't be an easy transition—in fact, quite the opposite. We will encounter an invasive species, the Raves!! Three years are left, and everything will be quite difficult, so prepare yourselves!! In fact, the cosmic history began in 2013, but the rebirth itself will unfold in a very mysterious and subtle way, and we must be in tune!! It will be a shocking rebirth, but at the same time, we will witness the fall of the empire and the collateral effects of an era's end that will have lasting consequences and will be very interesting, that's for sure!

Don't let your vanity or indoctrinated mindset prevent you from seeing or imagining your reality, which, until today, you've denied for many reasons; stop controlling your existence, flow with life, and update yourself. Think about preparing thoroughly—the present is relentless, it doesn't show mercy or contemplation; maybe you don't even sense it because you're simply playing the "wrong game," or have you already lost the will to care??!! Probably, everything you know right now doesn't allow you to breathe peacefully because you're disconnected from your nature; can you unlearn in order to update your mental set?? Don't doubt yourself, and doubt everything!!

Basically, you must stop wanting to control your life and be radical in your process. Rebirth is intense, and sometimes hostile!!

Are you exhausted, distracted, bored, alienated, and depressed?? You can always reinvent yourself—your life is what's at stake, and you have no choice!! It won't be an easy transition, that much is for sure, but you might have fun if you commit to being yourself, and not someone else!! Don't get distracted and don't let fear, indifference, or normality settle into your imagination… Don't lose your direction or sense of humor, you are absolutely perfect, fragile and vulnerable, but also a mess when trying to control life. Do you accept the challenge?? Being unique is inevitable, but not everyone can embrace the truth and take responsibility: free yourself from your egoic, vain, and controlling self, love yourself and surrender; enjoy your solitude, the Multiverse embraces you and celebrates your difference!!

At this point, we must do our best to understand, as we stand on the threshold of an era shift. We are closing and finalizing a very intense, transcendent moment. We've evolved up to here with navigation parameters and cultural coordinates that we all already know!! We are highly conditioned by a 7-shaped way of thinking, evolving within a 9-shaped framework, and thinking as though we are 7. We are in transition… from 7 to 9, mutating to a 9-center form!!

Basically, we must understand that we are just three years away, and there is little time left to reorient and accept that we are about to live through the most intense moment ever experienced on planet Earth. Emotionally, it's difficult to absorb and/or manage, mentally it's exhausting, and the frequency drops, whether from fear or a "non-self" resisting being. But it must be said that it is still exciting, the vertigo is noticeable!!

Do you know who you are when you wake up in the morning??

One can prepare to live in many ways, but your way of thinking is addictive and outdated by now; we've lived relatively well, but the imbalance is noticeable, and in such complex times, all forces come together, to

measure and also to **surpass** themselves!! Surpassing oneself requires a radical transformation, and acceptance. We are called to live through a historic, transcendently epic moment!!

We must understand that two eras are converging, and even the gods are coming to dance and enjoy this tragic, comic, and sublime moment. All living beings are being called to it, and we must rise to the occasion and be the best version of ourselves; freedom will make us free if we reinvent ourselves with love—there's no other choice!!

We are co-creators, and we've evolved to understand what's happening now. We must accept the challenge, whatever comes our way, we'll face it if we've absorbed and practiced what we truly are! It's not about what we know or think we know, but about understanding that we are mutating and taking a quantum leap, each of us—this is a change we must accept and integrate, each in our own way!! We're returning to conscious individualism!!?? It's inevitable if we want to grasp a macro/cosmic mutation!! Are we becoming aware, or not??

We must be able to enjoy this with those who find joy in their own joy, and at the same time, make it a game. Being yourself is quite fun, though I'm not saying it's easy. We've been so indoctrinated that the only thing left is love and humor to help us see what we sometimes don't want to see, or haven't stopped to see, because others control your time, and your mind.

To enter a world that will be very different, you don't need 3D glasses, because the movie is unfolding in another context and frequency… in fact, we are approaching the 5D, an internal and elemental journey to experience the Maia, or the very illusion itself; we are part of a game where you are both the protagonist and architect, if you choose. We are biohackers, transmuting to experience a type of reality according to personal coordinates that invite transcendence and interdependence. We are differentiating ourselves, or not!! Yes, we breathe life and amplify it with every breath in our singular and unique style… but we need to unlearn, because we have a thousand dependencies that prevent us from understanding and seeing what we could see. Open your eyes and get ready!!

Consciousness allows you to understand and assimilate your limits. We are filters of consciousness, self-reflecting consciousness!! All you need to do is place yourself in a space-time, and become aware of your form, in order to awaken, understand, and enjoy!! The body is what filters consciousness, the body is life—there's no choice!!

Prologue

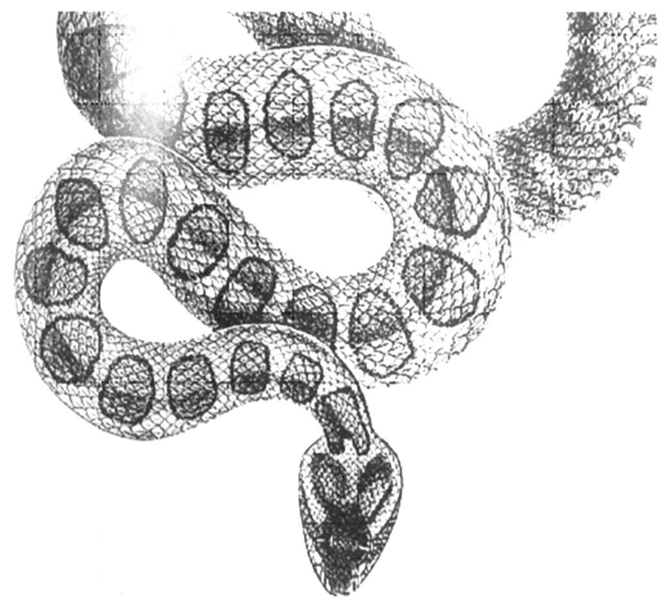

Certainly, abundance exists all day long, and it will continue to do so until infinity. The problem is that you and most human beings interfere with or try to control their reality in an obsessive, possessive, and alienating way, without realizing that everything is connected in a fractal manner—everything comes and everything mutates... The Age of Aquarius is ruled by Uranus, and everything is possible... You play a decisive role in this odyssey, but let's take it step by step, as we return to the origin and make a quantum leap!!

We can recognize and be reborn in an attempt or desire to reconnect with our essence. One only finds oneself by consciously diving into their holistic – hologenetic profile and recognizing, also, the Non-being; where we hold all our obsessions...

Mental patterns throw us into dimensions or contexts we can never control; here, we lose ourselves in a mental sea that, like a bubble, bursts with great ease, growing until it becomes unbearable anxiety, because we directly disconnect from our physical, emotional, or personal reality, which is in transferable. If one does not recognize their essence or form, they will keep searching and will never find their "character" or protagonist. It is essential to awaken and enjoy your own "performance," to recreate yourself in the character that, with time, learns to decide and live as well! It's evident that people don't know how to live, and it's not about money, but spirit!

Are you aware of the journey if you awaken and reinvent a world, your own, that today seems alien or alienating because it compares itself and denies itself? Remember that we are self-reflecting consciousness and fractally exist and evolve. Only in this way can we transcend our personal story and vibrate as one whole greater than the sum of its parts. If one is not conscious, they never will be. In fact, this consciousness holds and embraces us without measure, but one must be aware of oneself to filter the field of consciousness in which we live and, at the same time, program it with love.

We are co-creators, and rediscovery is not that difficult if one surrenders to the original form, where patterns and rhythms explain themselves. In fact, everything is quite simple if we learn to stop controlling life with the mind (we've always done it, and everyone does the same). This obsession is evidence, a compulsion of a world governed by Saturn, which is now decaying; it's time to return In the body, finding balance between the parts that truly take part, and playing. It's always now, but don't rush, recognizing the form takes time!!

Only if you awaken and rediscover yourself do you find yourself in a world that recognizes you through sympathy or symbiosis. Surrender means accepting yourself in all the circumstances of life, minute by minute. With every breath, we reconnect with ourselves each day, because deep down we are absolutely perfect if we center ourselves and align with natural rhythms, and stop interfering with the egoic, controlling, Saturnian, and anachronistic mind!!

Each one of us is singular and unique; in fact, we are neither aliens to the unfolding nor indifferent to the movement, but let's not obsess over changing ourselves to be someone else—that's a drama!! Everything changes constantly; we must learn to manage movement in a coherent and organic way, do you dance?? You don't have to change; if anything, you must dance and live with what you already are, even if you may have forgotten it. But how do you flow with a process of evident and wild mutation?! Only if you recognize yourself, accept yourself, and love yourself can you enjoy everything, and more!! You must know that it's a slow process, and it requires love for yourself!!

We are here to recognize our own story in an oasis of stars, planets, and parallel dimensions; it's time to seriously ask ourselves questions that can't be avoided if we stop to breathe consciously. A "reset" or a "shape-shifting" is needed, and also the desire to dance with life!!

Loving is quite easy because we are love, but we must first love ourselves in the absolute sense, even egoistically, without doubting our possibilities or abilities as thinking, living beings who walk to become the best version of ourselves, despite the differences and divergences. The question is almost unavoidable: why are people so afraid to be and/or "illuminate the world" with their presence?? Are you afraid to be who you are?? Yes!

The conviction one has of oneself is the result of the commitment one establishes with oneself? Being free presents a complex and sometimes hostile scenario, but why die of boredom when life is a cosmic joke, and you're playing at being yourself? Obviously, you must play, with both life and death, but you must understand to see!! You can't choose to be anything other than who you are, there is no choice!! Being someone else is a fraud that's outrageously expensive and embarrassing!! To find the original, you must die, reincarnate, and be reborn!! Being able to recognize yourself as unique and potentially marvelous is a privilege, possible and necessary, because there are only 3 years left until 2027. We are waves in a breathing sea, or fish in a river that gets lost in the vastness, and everything, absolutely everything, moves; and you, do you know who you are this morning? Who do you think you think you are??

Now you can get lost and return to the origin, safe travels!!

Prologue:
by Juryt Abma

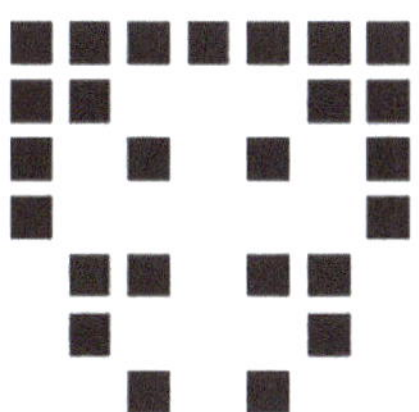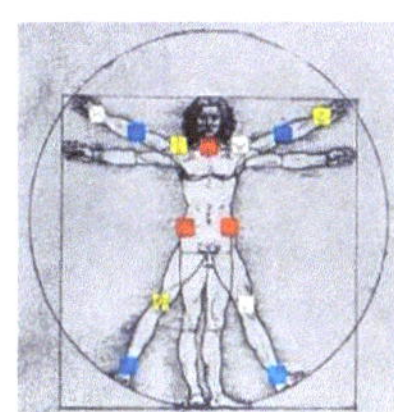

I hope that with this book, you have fun and enjoy the multidimensional experience. You can experience it as a game or as a journey, whichever feels best to you. You hold in your hands a unique and special book with which you can evolve and reinvent yourself. The second creation has already taken place, and the galactic synchronization too... With this book, you can understand more about certain future techniques that are deeply rooted in the past itself!! Understanding the codes is very interesting; numbers speak for themselves, they are divine creation!!

The ancient DNA system proposed by Human Design, with its 64 hexagrams in the Rave Mandala, is of great relevance; now we can learn to decode each hexagram within the cube.

U is the new DNA program of the new creation!!

The mysteries of U are many; in fact, it is like a game of chess on a board of 65 squares. Personally, I thank you for your support and your willingness to concrete... I am another You, someone who never stops dreaming, and in this dream, you are a cocreator just like me.

Molt teu, atentament:

Juryt Abma- Nit Blava Solar (kin 234)

3

Nosce te ipsum -
Oracle of Delphi:
Ad maiorem gloria globi

I will ask a trick question right at the beginning of the book: Do you deserve everything and more? Do you really deserve it, but you must understand that we're not going far, and everything is moving very fast; have you earned it? You don't even have to ask for it, but it doesn't just fall from the sky, although life sometimes surprises you if you are the one dancing with it, right? The question is whether one deserves access to abundance, and if one is prepared for what is inevitable, and what is desired... But don't ask for pears from the pear tree, and above all, be grateful; for now, thank the universe for making it possible for you to have this book in your hands, which will unfold in a polyhedral way wherever there is good people, light, and love... Now it's just a matter of you being yourself, and not someone else who lives mentally distracted, depressed, or alienated!!

Time puts everyone in their place, they also say time runs out, some say it doesn't even exist!! It is also true that time is spiral and that it's a factor that alters the mind. Don't let them control your mind or your life, or else you're already sold!!

Before we get into the subject, I want to make it very clear that my purpose is one: I wish for everyone to have the opportunity to make a quantum leap and return to the origin. It's time to breathe prosperity, wealth, vitality, and abundance, right? Remember, we are entering the Age of Aquarius, and we need to be aware that the possibility of creating a better and more conscious world comes from co-creating with love, but without forgetting the material aspect and the decadence we find ourselves immersed in!! Balance is needed, and we must reinvent ourselves!!

The spirit animates matter, it's evident, and the planet is awakening—or is it? Is it an illusion? It is real and happening, but in a subliminal or unconscious way, slowly... The rigor and obstinacy for matter (mater-matrix) are excessive; in any case, it lacks spirit, love, and generosity. The awakening is real, but almost imperceptible. On the other hand, everything is normalized, and everyone doubts everyone, but we are evolving at "forced marches" and it's not easy to catch the rhythm of it all. In fact, we don't even know where we are!!

Everything points to the fact that the "reality" we know is ending; it is a civilization sentenced… With elephant feet, we are witnessing the sinking of the Titanic, and I don't want to sound apocalyptic, but the facts speak for themselves!!

If we are not able to face the new world, it will be extremely difficult because the old one has very little credit left. State structures are faltering, and they are no longer sensitive or sustainable, nor even real… We've been made to believe that there is only one truth to live by, and we've forgotten about ourselves, the "I," the "you," and breathing!! The economy is showing obvious signs of exhaustion, but some still try to maintain the monopoly of an absurd, sometimes ridiculous religion. Yes, everyone knows it, but no one takes responsibility for the situation, for their own!! We continue with unconscious dependence and "delegating" to authorities that are either worthless or unemployed scapegoats!!

The game is over in 2027, are you ready?

Here ends the old world, and we'll see where we end up. It will change our mental construct, and the parameters of navigation will be different, very different, we can't even imagine!!

Let's be attentive to the effects of Uranus in direct motion in Gemini over the next 8 years, a relevant and revolutionary wake-up call. It must be said that Taurus' domains are matter, and Gemini's are communication.

Gemini is very versatile, and Uranus will leave the garden well transformed, and it will never be the same as before. In fact, we are already starting to see this. Obviously, there is awareness in certain areas, but the situation is exceptional and delicate. However, I feel that there's a lack of elegance, love, excitement, spirit, and the will to play… everything is too serious, and fear is not allowing us to breathe.

Infantilism, malpractice, and unconsciousness are perceived; there's a lack of emotional maturity, too much hypocrisy, and fear of losing control. In fact, there's a lack of imagination, critical thinking, and judgment. The worst of evils is indifference—it paralyzes great wills and drowns genius, innocence, and life!!

It's better to take some distance and wait. Everything will come, and with calm, we can decide; there is a lot of pressure for the imminent reality we will live in 2027, which, in fact, is tomorrow itself—everything is accelerating!! *The dark is coming!!*

I believe the awakening will be hard. Maybe the light entities will rescue us, or something like that... it's a possibility that also has its followers. Depending on how things unfold, it wouldn't be so bad, but maybe they don't want to know anything about us!!

Let's be "intelligent" and stop with the romance and fantasies because people are suffering a lot, and anything can happen, but the cautious man is worth two. I hear the bells ringing all day long, and doubled... as someone once said, it's better to tie the horses!!

It's evident—the excess of mental control that they "suggest" to us, the permanent dogmatism, the prejudices, the depression/frustration that is felt before and after Covid-19... it seems to lead us to a gray world heading towards black, right? It's the beginning of the end. It will be what it will be, and you will see it if you decide to be yourself and stop with the substitutes or mental addictions to avoid life itself; fear paralyzes, and it obsesses. If the stones could speak!!

So much indifference is insulting. The world produces poor people with money, wealthy ignorants, extreme rationalists without spirit or ethics, and poor-spirited individuals who live controlled and

manipulated!! Normalization knows no bounds; it's an epidemic that only brings misery!!

We are human beings trapped in a body that moves to the sound of a whistle, rejecting touch or avoiding eye contact. We barely raise our voices anymore, surrendered to vulgarity, obligation, mediocrity, and bad taste... Where are we heading?? Does it seem like a collective suicide??!! Self-sabotage?? Normalization!!

We must be optimistic and turn it around, right?

Let's be brave, let's be the best version of ourselves, and let's be authentic. Enough with the fakers and the traitors!!

You don't have to change or believe anything; you just have to want to be yourself and stop being a predictable subject, a victim of the Non-being, who only seeks to control what is not, with a full agenda of interests and soulless people who aim to control you!! Let's be irreplaceable and unique, let's return to the origin and reinvent ourselves, we have no choice!!

Let's put on a good face, or whatever face we have, take care of ourselves, water the garden, and truly play! Destiny is forged by making decisions and enjoying life; we cannot forget that life is given to us and deserves to be lived, respecting diversity, with self-love, and courage. Amor omnia vinci (love conquers all).

Loving your difference allows you to appreciate that of others. In fact, it's the only way to avoid the permanent conflict between equals/unequals... We cannot give in to normalization, nor to the Neocon dictatorship that plays at controlling the whole planet, and our destiny. All of this has led us to a perverse, ridiculous, and self-destructive capitalism-consumerism, a religion based on ignorance and a lack of consideration/love for nature... it seems that the Blue Planet is heating up quickly, just like your indoctrinated, normalized mind, eager for a thousand fantasies!! Simplify, "hack" your mind, update your mental set, and return to your body!!

I repeat, there are 3 years until 2027, after which we will face a rather unsettling scenario, and we will no longer be ourselves. I mean, the mutation we are experiencing is an evidence, and there are certain things we cannot avoid... Life, at times, surpasses all we can imagine or think!! Breathe, we will even witness the emergence of a new species, the Rave!!

Unsettling is an understatement; we will live with beings with a high degree of collective consciousness, "invaders," and autistic beings!! They are coming after 2027!!

4

Lakshmi, Goddess of Wealth, Royalty, and Freedom

The first thing to keep in mind regarding prosperity (a step beyond wealth) has to do with a personal attitude or predisposition and a way of understanding your life; yes, it involves living consciously with others in the very illusion of Maia, which keeps us "trapped" but which we cannot evade; we are the Maia, we are co-creators of realities and universes, some of us are already talking about the Multiverse without hesitation!! We are dreaming within a dream that is also dreaming us. Remember that the dreamer is more important than the dream itself, but let yourself dream, the universe has hidden tricks, wake up!!

The abundance of spirit invites us to live far from victimhood, we're talking about hexagram 55, a key that plays a decisive role before and after 2027: it says that individual knowledge brings us closer to freedom. Here, the great mutation of the species happens at an individual/egoistic level; one must know how to be, and how to freely coexist with the people around you, but most of all, it requires a personal commitment to your freedom, which will crystallize sooner or later if you learn to breathe yourself, for example, and enjoy yourself without fear... playing has its mystery and its risks too; awakening is a process, it's not immediate, it requires maturation and proper digestion; freedom also means knowing how to make the right decisions. We must understand that everything changes, but first, we need to recognize our own limits, and make a "shape-shifting," a change of form!! Only then do we place ourselves in space-time!!

We will have to address the most immediate and significant question; yes, we must answer who am I for myself outside of the social, cultural, and political construct where we are very trapped!! Who do I think I am?? What do I do alone with my own existence, what meaning or purpose do I have for life?

Maybe, over time, you will find that life has meaning after all, but don't let your guard down, the game of life is quite unsettling, and also dangerous!! We are interdependent, not soulless sheep surrendered to the apathy of a decaying civilization that causes indigestion and misery!!

Once you surrender to the form and look at things from a distance, you can evaluate the situation with perspective. We are passengers: you have no choice, you are unique and different, but you will have to start from the beginning, again!! You are not a soulless being without love, nor just another citizen feeding an obsolete (Egoic) system that no longer excites anyone… Remember that many children die of hunger on the planet, and many people can't even comprehend the degradation of the immune system; when defenses drop, everything becomes more complicated!!

Do you want to be a boring slave who directly becomes a victim of yourself? Or do you want to be an indoctrinated person obsessed with a small world that no longer works, even though it keeps spinning at a dizzying speed?? The awakening will be extremely harsh!!

Yes, the world is heating up at full speed, no one really knows what's happening, and if you don't breathe, you might have a mental diarrhea outbreak; you will remain trapped in a nightmare of freedom, whether it's given or imposed, that you don't even believe in anymore?? Once you gain enough clarity about how you are with yourself, you will begin to live and be a person, not a fish outside the fishbowl!!

Once you gain enough clarity about how you are with yourself, you will begin to live and be a person, not a fish outside the fishbowl!!

Human Design: The Science of Differentiation

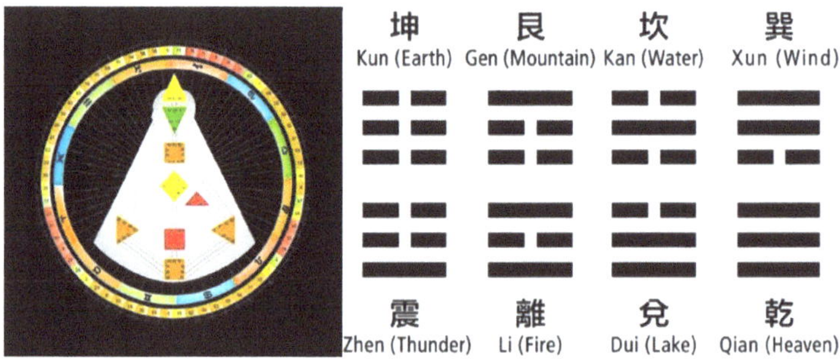

Human Design: It is the first modern science, a synthesis of knowledge that approaches the human experience in an integral way, an absolute: the first holistic, integral reference where the synthesis becomes an evident and understandable reality; an absolute that allows you to navigate with coherence and discover who you are!! Here, Vedic Astrology, the I-Ching, Quantum Physics, Kabbalah, and Biology merge. It is an integrated system of knowledge: the science of differentiation has its logic, a mechanism, and requires praxis… otherwise, you cannot dive deeper into the experiment!!

It is a tool of great depth to return to the body and experience in an organic and real way, it's not a theory!! Here, we embark on an odyssey of great beauty, a miracle, where you are the protagonist; it's neither a theory nor a dogma... it's the celestial chart specific to the Age of Aquarius, which is why we talk about a being with 9 centers, not 7 (Saturnian). We all represent an irreplaceable master formula that has its own mechanism, we're talking about a system that requires constant and/or radical praxis to provoke a mutation and a rebirth. It is here where Astrology itself is "surpassed" or transcended, becoming a unique reference that catalyzes modernity itself!! Here, we have the conscious/unconscious binomial delineated… Yes, we are binary consciousness with a center of direction (magnetic monopoly) and love! We are love, but the mind does not allow us to understand such a simple fact, and this geometry gives us direction!!

We are talking about an absolute, approaching a form that confirms our absolute perfection, as long as there is commitment and dedication; making decisions is crucial for becoming aware and evolving. We can say that the mind does not decide, on the contrary, the mind has a specific cognitive function but no authority. The body is a filter of consciousness, it is the vehicle, or a temple, that has memory, and a specific vibration!!

Ra Uru Hu, the messenger and mystic, illuminates us with a synthesis of great transcendence, a shocking, supernatural intelligence; its simplicity is infinite, but not everyone can understand its depth unless they approach it correctly. It requires patience and love!!

His message would deserve 8 Nobel Prizes (academics still haven't understood it, because they would be exposed, or perhaps they don't want you to be yourself); it seems that it's not in the interest for this knowledge to reach so many people, who are kept indoctrinated with fear, ignorance, and media violence all day long. Remember, you represent yourself, and you signify daily, you are who you are, but you must tune in and adjust…

you need to get into orbit, recognize your truth… and let those who understand you "buy into it," as my father used to say!!

One must know how to be alone and leave space for others to take their place, understanding and unlearning takes time!! Only if you are the one who manifests or reproduces yourself, will you be perfectly recognized and valued. The rest will come by synchronicity, basically depending on your commitment to the experiment of being yourself; trust life, everything has its process, you must persevere, be very devoted to yourself, and not accept substitutes or poor imitations. We are free to doubt everything, there is no clean slate, so tie up the horses well and open your eyes, don't swallow a "gripaU"!!

I prefer to dance with life and enjoy while the body is capable of seeing the wonder of attending an unprecedented spectacle, because in the end, you recognize yourself in the whole, and that makes you immensely rich and fortunate!! Being yourself means many things, remember that it is in adversity where challenges appear and where one measures themselves against themselves; not everyone takes responsibility for this, they prefer to obey and follow the mandates of the Diputació or the Vatican, who "let us think and all," all very rational, official, and outdated!! In my view, we think too much, and since we don't know how to think, we get tangled in a conditioned and normalized reality, which ultimately becomes a "virtual and online" mental game, regulated by cultural institutions indoctrinated to maintain control over a "messianic" discourse, disconnected from nature, and without spirit!! Think that the universe conspires in favor of you if you are *You*, but against you if you are a normal person!!

Yes, knowing how to enter requires a real commitment to your world and to life; only then do solutions, combinations, and possible scenarios appear, but also rationalist detractors trapped in an ego that has stopped playing to become a victim, and/or an alienated controller.

In fact, we are here to be ourselves and to know who we are; you won't deny yourself this adventure, right? Reinventing oneself is possible, but it requires "dying" and being reborn!! One thing you need to know to make this journey is the position of Pluto in your Rave chart. Your densest truth may prove essential to not lose your way, and there are only 3 years left until 2027!!

The demand or commitment to oneself marks the difference, strengthens, tones, and brings us closer to Olympus, to Parnassus, or to Eden!! If you have let yourself down or have failed, don't hesitate to forgive yourself, it's a good start. I remind you that all of this will take a Copernican turn in 2027, and we will find ourselves in a very different scenario!! You've already surrendered with windmills and with the evolutionary program, which is relentless, and frankly, it cares very little about you; you are very tired, and also scared!!

This text seems to invite us on a deep journey of self-awareness and personal acceptance, emphasizing the importance of not controlling, but rather learning to enjoy the simple act of being oneself. It refers to the concept of *Human Design,* a tool that combines various esoteric systems to help us understand our true nature and how we interact with the world. The text highlights that each of us is unique, and our inner formula is key to deciding how to live with coherence, using our own strategies and internal authorities.

The central idea seems to be liberating ourselves from mental limitations, leaving behind conditioned realities and the "normality" that often leads us to ignorance. It encourages reflection on the fact that we are interdependent and that everything is connected, but the answer lies within ourselves. The path isn't easy, but it's about becoming aware, taking the first step, and continuing to play, making the most of each moment.

The text also mentions the duality of the universe and the mechanics that govern it, inviting us to learn to "dance" with life, following our own rhythm, with patience and distance, in order to gain a clearer and deeper view of ourselves and the world around us.

It seems to be a powerful message for those seeking a profound shift in how they understand life, the body, and the mind. A reminder that, despite the challenges, we are responsible for our own evolution, and the path to authenticity may be complicated, but it's also full of beauty and growth.

Let's take it step by step, prepare yourself consciously, making decisions is **determinant** and marks the difference; your journey is **unique**, personal, and non-transferable!! You are alone, and everything is okay, but remember, your traveling companions have also gotten lost, they live in an alienated world, and everything is moving!!

Yes, you must learn to be alone, find good company, recognize who is in your life's fractal, trust yourself, because you are not here to control or choose your friends or travel companions, they simply appear and disappear!! Hacking your mind is always possible, in fact, it is desirable at this point, and above all, **don't let anyone tell you what to do**, enough already!!

The first step is always the hardest, but you'll have to take it yourself, alone; through difficulty, one matures and evolves. Not doing it would be fatal!! Yes, it's a **personal and non-transferable decision**, but if it weren't difficult, it wouldn't really be worth starting, right? Difficulty forges character, are you ready??

We are living in very exciting times, with great intensity; the complexity is evident, and simplifying is necessary if you want to **unlearn**, understand, and decide for yourself in a world that recognizes no one, a world that is disappearing and fragmenting, it's a mess!!

Emotions today play a key role in the transpersonal socio-economic dynamic. In the Solar Plexus, there is a substantial change occurring, the species mutation goes through the management of these emotions; when there is chemistry, there is transformation, and the vibration rises, then falls, it's cyclical and of great intensity, however, they invite us to **become conscious**!!

It takes a certain amount of patience to assimilate the mutation and find clarity. I can already tell you that managing emotions has its complexity; in fact, this is where the final battle is fought. Be brave, look your best, don't forget your wallet, and stop thinking like most people, who hide among the herd and disguise it poorly!! What I mean is that reality doesn't exist until we confront it, enjoy it, and assimilate it… reality needs a conscious protagonist!

If you start over, they won't make it easy for you. No one said that the art of living is easy, but it is an art in itself if we take on the commitment to *be*. Don't let yourself be controlled, we've denied ourselves too much already, and we've been tricked by the system, by both sides!!

Step back to see your own movie. Little by little, you'll make your way, and stop being the one who wanted to control and be normal. Normality and comparison are a collective fraud, a farce!! One day, you'll see everything fall into place. The competitors or detractors will disappear, you'll forget them, and everything will take on a dimension somewhere between real and paranormal, and apples will taste like apples.

If you trust yourself, you've already won a lot, but if you're not radical, they'll make you fall on your face, and since they're "few" and cowards, they'll laugh at you… or maybe not!!

Think that right now, everyone is full of fear, and if you're a stranger or a wolf, they'll probably want to cancel you because your vulnerability is very tempting. Be alert and keep your eyes open, because in the vineyard of the Lord, there's everything. However, you can always disappear or learn to be invisible!!

Human Design/BG5: This is a subsystem or component of Human Design that works with auras, trans personally, to manage human resources or groups of people. It is a consulting system designed to optimize resources and energies. Managing energies also has its own mystery!

It analyzes the collective while also addressing individual aspects, so improvement is significant, respecting each individual's nature and coordinating synergies and complementarities between people. A work team today needs to understand how the energies and dynamics of each person work. If everyone's individuality is not respected, it becomes very difficult to motivate or help each person find their place within the company, community, or organization. The "Pentes" are groups of people working together towards a common goal.

To gain consistency, it is essential to respect differences. Each person has their own resources and genuine potential that the team must know how to manage. Moving from hierarchy to hierarchy, where everyone takes on conscious individual responsibilities, requires a comparative analysis to place each person in a real and understandable context. It is necessary to understand the environment in which we are moving in order to act more efficiently and precisely.

The Penta and the chemistry between team members are fundamental concepts within Human Design/BG5. The Penta refers to a group of people working together, and the chemistry between its members is key to understanding how these individual parts contribute to the whole. As it's said, "the whole is greater than the sum of its parts," it's important to understand how each part, or individual, functions separately before seeing how it connects and contributes to the whole.

Each person brings unique energy and a set of talents to the team, and it's essential to know what these strengths are in order to manage them properly and coordinate them with others. When each team member is understood and respected for what they bring individually (both in terms of personality and energy), it creates a dynamic that allows the group to be much more efficient and harmonious.

The idea that everything is connected and linked organically means that each interaction between team members is not random, but follows a logic of synergy and complementarity. When both individual and collective dynamics are understood, the team can function as a coherent unit where individual contributions are enhanced, and the whole is greater than the sum of its parts. This not only improves efficiency but also the well-being of everyone involved, creating a natural synergy that facilitates achieving common goals.

In short, managing a Penta means knowing how to identify each individual's resources and roles to create an organization where differences and complementarities between members are valued and enhanced, leading to a highly effective and cohesive group

It's interesting to observe other mutations of Human Design; of course, it has its detractors and different interpretations that can be equally compelling. Even though some may distort the original system, I'd like to think there are people who have "improved" or refined the interpretation, or perfected a science of individuation or differentiation, where the subject evolves in relation to different parameters or criteria.

Baantu posits that we are essentially robots subjected to an evolving program that constantly mutates and modifies us. In essence, it reminds us that we have no real choice—we are binary consciousness (conscious/unconscious, mind and body). In any case, the program keeps us in a dance that can either be macabre or incredibly dull if we fail to assimilate aspects of ourselves and open up to multidimensionality, primarily to be able to assimilate, understand, and navigate under adverse conditions.

The truth is, as we approach the end and the beginning of an era, everything becomes exceedingly unsettling—especially if you don't have certain knowledge about yourself. What does the universe want from you? What are you telling the cosmos while you breathe? What is your relationship with others beyond commerce, self-interest, and the game of egos? In reality, few people know "that they don't know," and resist life, which at times is very clear and generous. The majority live with a conditioned mental set, limited by being indoctrinated, deceived, or alienated, to varying degrees.

The Genetic Keys:
The Middle Path. Hologenetic Profile, 3 Sequences

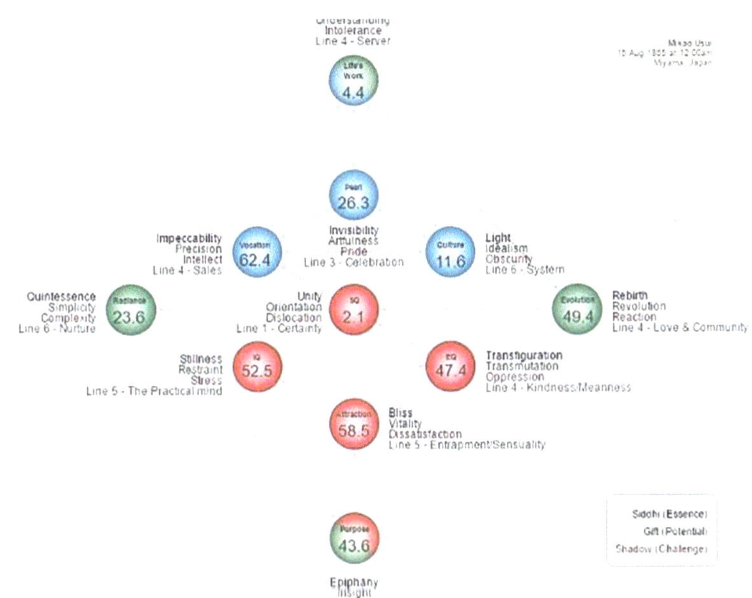

The Genetic Keys, by Richard Rudd: here we encounter an approach of great subtlety, and it's truly a mystery to enter and live out your hologenetic profile. In fact, it is an evolved version of Human Design. This approach works with the I-Ching, the ancient Chinese book, the

Kabbalistic Tree of Life, and three sequences. It suggests a forgotten mystical practice, the contemplation of the keys helps to activate and awaken our DNA through neurolinguistic programming and/or epigenetics. This accelerates the process of regeneration/mutation and represents a more Yin path.

Here we encounter a mysterious pattern of great beauty that unfolds with patience and love. We can say that it is the Yin version of Human Design, in fact, the approaches are very different in their focus!

We can approach the profile both analogically and digitally. It consists of activating a hidden potential within our genes, which, according to the reading, raises the frequency... Perhaps you are trapped in low vibrational states that make it difficult to heal and evolve? It's essential to recognize some truths and realities about oneself. After 2027, everything will be very different and complicated—there are 5 years left, and tough years are coming!

We are trapped in mental and physical victimhood and easily distracted, but we can decode and reactivate our DNA with love... You can recover your vital tone by contemplating the keys that most influence your evolution and transmute your worldly experience. Yes, becoming Homo Sanctus is a possibility that requires courage and real commitment!

Consider the possibility of knowing who you are and living the mystery itself, where consciousness is an infinite source of life! The mystery is a source of inspiration, and approaching your journey with the relevant keys can be truly beautiful. Don't forget that you've come to be yourself, and this implies a certain dialogue with your higher self, and/or your super ego!

Depeche Mode sings *Personal Jesus*, so settle in and try to assimilate your life's cross… prepare yourself to activate 3 sequences; as you recognize certain patterns, you also relax and accept what you already are, and one day, you no longer want to be anything else. Only then can you be alone or accompanied! There's a coming together of parts as you learn to be alone, a true challenge that doesn't mean being isolated! Simply put, you avoid dependencies or realities without spirit!

One day, the dance begins… The Activation Sequence is the first step. Don't deny or resist, it would be very sad, it's not too difficult, but you have to move your feet, your legs, and your ears. When you least expect it, the mutation, transmutation, or symbiosis occurs… or illumination, and then you can't stop dancing! You'll know what music moves you, but remember, it's the body that lives life.

You must live the process and confirm it for yourself. Self-illumination is a neo-narcissistic experiment of a mystical order (*The Genetic Keys* by Richard Rudd is a huge book and also a great investment). It's a memorable book that can be reread in a thousand ways since it has a life of its own—let yourself be surprised!

Yes, you can shine with your own light even in the darkness. Don't let them extinguish you because today you're gambling with your life if you stay in the new normality; don't slack off. Sometimes the wind blows in your favor, but at times, the wind blows against you if you're "a member of a mentally abducted and normalized entity"… The one who warns is not the tractor!

Discover your truth and accept the consequences, this way your mind will work in service of your self. Learn to think—this alone makes you immensely rich, and each day you need less energy, fewer things/resources, and you become more receptive because you understand that life is simpler, and you can dance with it if you enjoy it without needing to align with the priests and nuns who guide you to embrace *their* truth. In fact, we all think alike and even eat alike, and that's why we don't digest well and complicate our existence. A large part of the secret lies in knowing how to manage your personal energy, which determines how you move in space-time!

Unlearn and confront your truth, listen to yourself and love yourself; others may buy into it, or not; if it's your truth that resonates, people will recognize it, you will amplify it wherever you go, and you no longer need to be a hypocrite or a "snake-oil salesman" every day; being yourself is easier and more entertaining. If you live someone else's life, sooner or later you will face the wrath of God!!

Are you available and ready?? You need to know how to enter and also exit... Living a differentiated self is always better from a distance... however, if you enter the center of the hurricane, surprisingly you disappear, you become invisible, you can recreate or reinvent yourself... If you are in your place, you breathe with the infinite and apples fall from the sky, but you must open your eyes and hands, we are interdependent, but we all resonate with a melody, sometimes it sounds tuned, sometimes it resonates, and depending on how it goes, it becomes a symphony!! It's like entering a black hole, anything can happen… if you are ready, the experience will be cosmic, magical, and real; if life gives you apples, make apple juice, and if it gives you marijuana, you are very lucky, make cakes, and have a costume party!!

If you connect with your geometry, you will tie things together, touch the sky, or maybe open a wine cellar on the most unexpected day—who knows! I wish Dionysus accompanies you through the vineyards and shows you paradise, anything can happen, but you'll leave your comfort zone and have an experience that you can either explain or not; some things can't be explained because people wouldn't believe them, and that's okay; we are of a paranormal order, but the vast majority find refuge in a televised normality, lamentable, mediocre by nature… without a soul, you can't live!! You don't have to explain everything either, just be yourself and love yourself, but if you don't realize this, nothing will become plausible, fascinating, or remarkable. You must realize it, then you will gain awareness; it's a matter of practice and self-love!

What you don't give, as Jodorowsky wisely says, will be taken from you!! We could say it's about entering a game of exchange of monetary and emotional energies, without prejudices… if it's unconditional, even better, because there is no guilt, but be grateful, giving thanks is important and easy!! Yes, money is "positive" energy depending on where you've invested it; if you don't have it, I believe it's negative energy because your mind has to find a way to reverse a situation that sometimes is absurd, and sometimes necessary; we all learn to be and live in a wheel that turns, but this wheel needs "gasoline" and love.

I'm talking about managing your energy; you need to know how to be and walk through life… if you manage it consciously, you'll find you have more time to dedicate to the people you truly love… and that's priceless. If you have time, you're rich, but if they control your time, they control your mind, your life, and then you've already lost!!

Yes, you need to find a solution as soon as possible… you can't waste time; time is the most precious thing we have, and we must make the most of it, enjoy it, and manage it with imagination; the galactic culture already says it, Time is Art (13:20, the natural frequency of time), creating generates abundance, love, and life. But you need to know where we are and what the "currency" of change is if we want to actively participate in the game, which at times can seem like a colossal nonsense, but you're always in time to be the protagonist of your own movie, what more do you want?? If you live it your way, the doors will open, and others will close, obviously.

It's a formula that may seem cryptic, but we can understand it if we enter the dynamic of the 13-moon calendar... Take the first step, and once you're in the dynamic, you can understand the codes of the Law of Time, and things happen that no one imagines; synchronicity-symphony can be a miracle, in fact, you yourself are a miracle, riding a bike on a full moon night while two frogs make love!!

Are we talking about a meaningful life experience? Synchronicity!! Do you reinvent yourself every day? Remember, each day is new, every day the sun rises, and each day is different if you know how to be the protagonist and assume your role as a co-creator-inventor. Only then will you find synergies; being the protagonist isn't about being the best or the most applauded, it means you've understood your role within a macrocosm where you can flow. Are you the architect of your life?? If you play with love, you'll encounter universes or realities you never imagined. I know, from nothing comes flowers, or rabbits… in fact, we come from nothing, let's talk about the Big Bang, or 2027? According to Ra, the Big Bang is the result of a collision between two crystals, one yin and the other yang, which gave rise to the conception of the universe, which is still being conceived, it's in constant expansion, and we too are constantly evolving, but sometimes we involute to remember, especially now that we are approaching the end of an Era, and everything is starting to fail. That's why it's vital to return to the body!!

This perspective emphasizes the importance of understanding yourself as an active creator in the universe, where synchronicity plays a role in guiding you toward your true potential. We are in a state of continuous change, and it's a matter of aligning with that flow, both internally and externally, to navigate the evolution we're all a part of. Does this view resonate with you?

We are like an enigma or a formula that we are now beginning to understand with quite a bit of precision, but we come from nothing, and everything changes, and you need to stop wanting to control your life?? It's the best thing you can do... Now you are immersed in an odyssey, by 2027 everything will take a significant turn, and it's essential to be in tune with your higher self or super ego... Maybe you don't know who you are in the morning, or you're a fish out of water!!

Yes, miracles exist, they are the result of a real paranormal adventure, but you have to open your eyes... miracles have a lot to do with hexagram 35 (Progress, the ancient version of the I-Ching: it says that the King leaves 3 horses every day so he can go explore unknown worlds, an adventure to gain awareness); hexagram 22 also speaks of grace and miracles. Don't be miserable, as a strong wind might come and leave you without shelter, and without shoes, but fortunately, Neptune is at door 36... a door of humanism and compassion.

Yes, we all know, misfortune is no joke, but if you fall into grace, the doors of love can swing wide open!! And you, do you know who you are in the morning? You probably have no idea, I'd bet a shoe and my ears that sparkle!! You still haven't seen anything because you were looking through glasses prescribed by an alienated technocrat, and you couldn't stop, or integrate!! Try to breathe, the journey is eternal, you just have to flow, and trust yourself!!

The Genetic Keys is a poetic version of the Book of Changes (I-Ching), a necessary multidimensional journey; we're talking about a mystical and scientific version that will be very useful for understanding and living a

5D evolutionary process. The middle path is contemplative, to awaken your DNA, however, I suggest an author who works with the 12 layers of the code, a lemurian who delivers transcendental and very exciting teachings—Elan Cohen is Kryon: *The 12 Layers of DNA*.

This passage speaks to the idea of embracing life's natural flow, letting go of control, and recognizing the synchronicities and miracles that arise when we are open to the journey. It encourages us to explore our own inner landscape, understand our multidimensional nature, and trust in the process of spiritual and evolutionary awakening. The suggestion of Kryon's teachings and the 12 layers of DNA emphasizes the importance of self-awareness and transformation in the context of an ongoing, expansive spiritual journey. Does this resonate with your own journey?

As human beings/sapients in transition, we become *Homo Sanctus* aboard what we know as the ship of time, Earth!!

Yes, we are the Earth, and we must take care of it to be able to harvest the fruits and flowers that will pollinate the land, the place where we are meant to live, along with our children!! What a gift it is to walk barefoot and see spring arrive, right? Love it unconditionally, the mystics recognize it as the ship of time!! One land, one people, and one time: the natural frequency of time is 13:20... Ready for synchronicity?

Now enjoy time, savor time, and don't waste it on nonsense or things that aren't true. We can't waste time on misery and nonsense!! We must be prepared and receptive, love your truth, and enjoy whenever you can, consciously, because they want you distracted and scared!!

Welcome to your own personal or transpersonal odyssey; life isn't easy for anyone, but make it easy if you can, settle in, and flow in the immediate present. Without rush, we'll go far, or just to the corner to see how nameless green stars fall. One day, we'll meet again in a garden known as Eden. You're already there if you open your eyes... in fact, you can enter paradise with a set of keys you already hold in your hands. Walk!!

This passage encourages us to embrace our connection to Earth and time, to live consciously and in harmony with the natural rhythms around us. It's a reminder that the present moment holds the key to profound transformation and peace. The idea of *Homo Sanctus* points to a higher state of being, where we transcend the mundane and align with a greater, more sacred purpose. The keys to paradise are metaphorical tools for awakening—your awareness and intentionality are what unlock it. Does this message resonate with your own sense of purpose or journey?

The *Pearl Sequence* is the work of Richard Rudd; here, we release prosperity with simplicity!! The four stages of the holistic sequence of THE PEARL are: vocation, culture, brand, and the pearl; the pearl is right at the center, represented by Jupiter on the *Carte du Ciel*, where your quantum leap takes place... and unlimited abundance!!

The sequence describes a process of reorientation and synchronicity that connects you with the people, cultures, places, and dimensions necessary for your higher destiny to unfold. By representing a great blossoming in your life, the pearl delivers the secrets of prosperity through the personification of simplicity. We are talking about three dynamics that favor a quantum leap of your being if you embrace your law, represented by Jupiter.

In this stage, the entire journey becomes integrated as you experience yourself as a vibrant and unique facet within the geometry of wholeness... holistic!!

It would be wise to visit www.lasclavesgeneticas.com and search for your hologenetic profile, and live the Pearl Sequence, which catalyzes a real dynamic of prosperity!

The *Venus Sequence* allows us to understand and live our relationships in a singular and poetic way!! Here, there are 6 centers or gates to work with love and patience, as relationships deserve that!!

The activation sequence connects us with our life's purpose, but there is no definitive purpose; at some point, it manifests and seduces you… There are no answers or reasons you can control or manipulate with your supposed intelligence. "Your freedom" will take you to where you need to be. Don't force things by speculating about realities that don't exist, or that only exist in your mind. You must integrate and embody; in the end, it has to resonate at an internal level!!

Simply enjoy the journey, be present, and enjoy being invisible; you are alive and wonderful, fall in love with yourself, you have no choice, you are absolutely perfect, what more do you want??

Yes, you are the great love of your life. Don't let your soul control what you are not, and what you do not want to be!! Life will come to find you, and so will death!! Four frogs with duck feet will also come to dance at your funeral… everything is an illusion. Mysteriously, everything becomes what it is if you open your eyes, and your mind!! Remember, there are 3 years left, and you need to be prepared because we'll dance, laugh, and sweat like never before. You can't even imagine!!

Dear, beloved, and unknown young spirit, boys and girls who dream of omelets or the very vastness itself, let the mystery embrace you and ask you the right questions. You'll find answers when you look into the mirror, which you'll find in a drawer where a Russian tailor is dancing the sardana. Don't obsess over changing too much, everything changes. One day, you might even recognize yourself when you wake up in the morning as an unlimited original version with a good hand, two ears, and a desire to dance!!

Yes, you are absolutely perfect with your imperfections, and with a personal purpose that seeks you out every day!! Don't be foolish and stop chasing ideals or impossibilities; your head is full of sparrows and frogs. Unlearn every day and never stop dreaming, because the dream also dreams you!! It's always now, and if you want your freedom, don't stop breathing. Life is relentless, but also a sweet melody—bitter and cruel, but every day the Sun rises…

God loves you if you laugh at yourself every day, but don't lose your way, and keep walking, because the path goes up!! If you stop walking, you might find yourself and have a "patatUs" (a mental block), or a "telele" (a dizzy spell)!! Do you understand?? While you walk, your thoughts align… the gerund allows us to understand a present that always evokes a past (where we come from), and maybe one day it will become a wonderful future!

Everything is very doubtful and mysterious, but don't take it too seriously because victimhood doesn't serve you, and complaining doesn't either… There's too much pretense and nonsense in serious postures that imply normality, and boredom!! Mutation does not allow excuses or justifications. It's a *work in progress* or an adventure… You have no choice!!

The Tzolkin and the Law of Time

With Dr. José Argüelles (Valum-Votan), a great 5,200-year cycle is coming to an end. His work invites us to live in a truly magical world, full of beauty and harmony, where time has a natural frequency (13:20) that frees us from the mental slavery and control imposed by a mechanical time system (12:60), which was introduced by the Vatican in the form of a calendar. This calendar remains deeply embedded in our collective imagination and even in our DNA!!

It is essential to understand that time is the factor that changes our mental perception of reality. If we are in the wrong frequency, we can easily be abducted and manipulated, which is exactly what has been happening since the moment they stole our time. Yes, they stole our time, and we need to enchant ourselves again!!

We must also recognize that we are traveling in a time ship, and time is circular or elliptical, not linear, which alters the parameters of navigation. We are within a matrix of 260 kins (the 260-day cycle of the Tzolkin), which allows us to think and live within a harmonic mental construct. The Synchronary/13 Moon Calendar has an organic rhythm and beauty... Here, we are talking about the planetary mind and the Noosphere!! Synchronizing ourselves and understanding cosmic science will be part of a journey where the possibilities are infinite if you recognize your place and your role in the grand scheme of things. Telepathy is the science of the future!!

Dr. José Argüelles - Valum Votan (11:11 - Blue Monkey 11) presents us with a game, a journey, a multidimensional illusion... where peace and culture become a binomial that synchronizes us with natural time!!

Shall we talk numbers? Mystical mathematics, or *mathemagics*, is the result or explanation of the Law of Time (13:20, Time is Art), where time is spiral, reinvented, or recreated!! Argüelles also left us with the *Chronicles of Cosmic History*, a scientific treatise that deserves much attention and dissemination. It's not easy reading, but there are good translations, and some of his disciples continue to address a subject that is already beginning to be recognized, enjoyed, applauded, and followed by those who are familiar with the 13 Moon Synchro nary, the Tzolkin, or the Telektonon!!

Dear crew member of the time ship, on July 26, 2013, something known as the Galactic Synchronization or Second Creation took place.

It was a very significant turning point to understand that the cosmic history has just begun. The Galactic Culture is the culture of wholeness, light, consciousness, and peace, which are essential and decisive parts of our journey as Earth's crew members. Here, we are all magicians and essential cocreators. In fact, we are witnessing a quantum-evolutionary leap of dimensions still to be understood, and we must prepare ourselves; it is a collective ascension that raises the level of consciousness of the collective, where the planetary mind begins to take shape… are we talking about the Noosphere?!! Here, telepathy reconnects us all in an organic and playful way, where the mind transcends the Technosphere and activates with the heart. Here, we begin to navigate as an intelligent and holistic collective (of wholeness), leading us to a shift in mentality and perception!!

At the cellular level, this mutation is also taking place, and we must be aware of it. In fact, it's a process of synchronization with the Maia; be free within infinite possibilities, but learn to think, and to cultivate the art of living! You can experiment with your archetype or galactic seal… By changing the frequency of our DNA, we also change the aura or vibrational field that we emit all the time, which we must understand and take care of. The aura manifests or expresses itself more intensely when we are aware and in harmony with ourselves… By playing with consciousness, we learn to navigate and to live; this is also true with emotions, which are amplified with every breath, creating a personal and collective reality at the same time. The Noosphere, the planet's aura, will help us save planet Earth if we work in teams, and with love; everyone must find their team or galactic circle where they can experience and/or live a game, which is also a planetary dream!!

Right now, the field is almost defeated, divided, and trending toward victimization. There is a chronic state of apathy and dependence, in every sense; it's clear that people don't love themselves, they've lost telepathic connection, and the relationship with others, who also don't know that they don't know. Vanity consumes you like a "product" or alienated mercantile subject without a soul, desperately seeking happiness or freedom, without taking into account the connection with the Noosphere, the "planetary mind." The mind gets busy looking for subterfuges or artificial realities that serve to keep us deceived, all the result of repeated obsessive thoughts that aren't true... Many people prefer to live deceived; are we talking about sabotage or collective suicide??

Self-esteem is very low because the lie is pharaonic; people don't trust themselves, nor do they trust life, and they repeat mechanisms/patterns. Obviously, the results are dependence, spiritual, economic, and emotional poverty... In the Technosphere, permanent inequality, malpractice, and an abusive use of energetic and/or emotional resources are experienced! This leads us to a state that is unappealing, unfriendly, implausible, and of great complexity... turbulent times are coming, 2027 is approaching inexorably, can you feel it??!!!! Everyone perceives it in one way or another, but the mind is obsessive and wants to control, hence the anxiety and the state of collective neurosis!! There is nothing to control, in fact, it's necessary to understand and assimilate in order to enjoy and co-create.

It's better to be yourself and walk, whether or not others like your modus operandi. You have a geometry and a vibration that takes you where you need to go... stop overthinking with a mistaken ego, in a hostile environment!! You can always disappear or enter dynamics of infinite prosperity, don't let your subconscious limit you!!

Are we returning to the origin? This is the story we are meant to live, the new one, but we must go through the transition and manage a past that continues to be visible, reminding us where we come from and who we are. In order to mutate, we need to have a self and a past. Take a breath, flow, and play at being yourself, but without forgetting that the other is part of the enchantment, a likeness or an entity with its own life! We are mutating, you are a genius and perhaps you don't know it... You need to wake up, get into position, place yourself in a "real" context where you can truly be yourself, and disappear if the music doesn't align. Everything changes, this is a journey we are all taking together, each at our own pace, and it's just beginning..

Yes, you are chosen or privileged, you are unique, unrepeatable, singular, and different. You are not special, nor should you compare yourself to anyone else. You must love yourself consciously and without excuses because, deep down, you are perfect if you accept who you are! You just need to internalize, reproduce, and perfect your galactic KIN... you don't need to change anything, just get to know your essence and be the best version of yourself. Throughout the journey, you will stop being who you are not, or who they made you believe you are! Fair winds, and a new boat!

If you doubt yourself too much, others will keep doubting you, always, and it will be much harder to find your place/game; learn to live and see with your own eyes. Right now, it may feel like the wind is against you, but soon you'll face a tremendous storm—I warn you! Anything can happen. We will live some very exciting moments, but don't resist it. I suppose you already know that this is not a local festival, it's a *festival*, but you'd better open your eyes! In bad weather, put on a good face, a sense of humor, and love, because loving strengthens you and says a lot about who you are—*a lot!* But don't let anyone tell you how to love; love however you want, and don't forget to be as different as you can and want. Diversity will thank you infinitely, and so will we!

Being different means you cannot compare yourself to anyone, do you get it? You are neither better nor worse; you are absolutely perfect, you are *unique*, amazing! You are very lucky, and you have no choice!

In this web of doors and channels, I want to remind you of key number 26 because it activates the thymus gland, which is vital for health: Hexagram 26 speaks of the power of taming the great, of surrendering to the great master plan!! The divine plan is an act of co-creation, and a great game, not an alienating doctrine that generates fear in people!! In Kabbalah, 26 would be a significant sacred number; when summed up, it becomes 8, infinity… a number revered by the Chinese, and a sign of abundance!!

The great truths are also subject to interpretation, even time deserves to be revisited and reconsidered; we interpret it as a linear and mechanical reality because, at one point, it was stolen and imposed by the Vatican, and that's how the world went! We've been swindled, and our time has been stolen! The Age of Aquarius is marked by Uranus, which will be the planet that opens us to a new understanding of time, which until now has been heavily influenced by Cronus-Saturn!

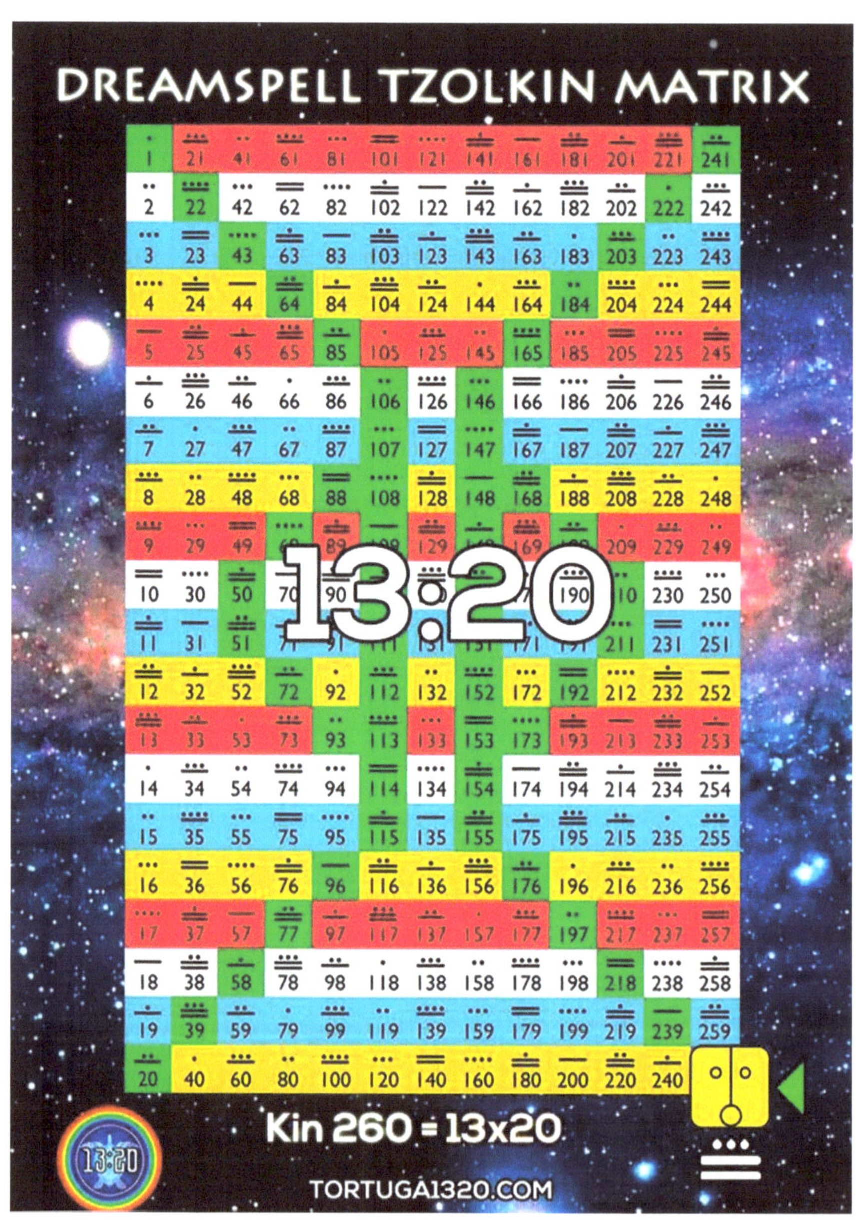

The Harmonic Module

U-Ching: the new DNA program of the human being; a book of codes

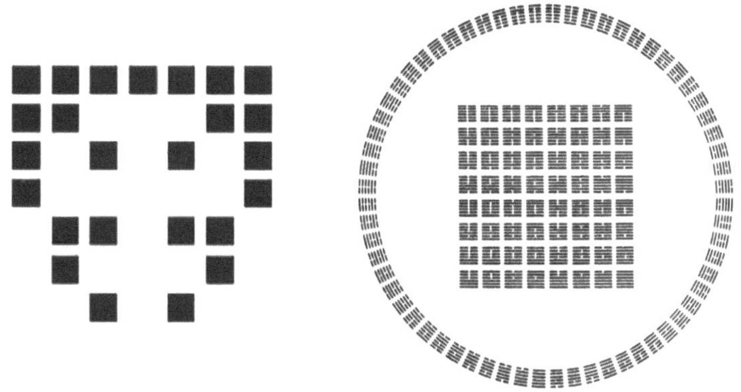

On July 26, 2013, a great mutation occurred, the I-Ching mutated into itself and became the U-Ching!! We're talking about a book of codes, mathemagics or mystical mathematics, the new DNA program!! A calendar synchronized with the Tzolkin; a work by Juryt Abma, translator of Argüelles and of the 7 volumes of the Chronicles of Cosmic History!!

Yes, I want to make it known that the I-Ching has mutated, the U-Ching is a miracle in itself!! It is a miracle because it is an extraordinary mutation... the book of changes or mutations mutates into itself!! Changes imply a separation-division/duality-dynamic tension of some specific reality. It's interesting to observe a millennial pattern and its mutation, a dynamic reality that keeps us alive... We're talking about the Oracle of the Tao and a pattern that allows us to synchronize with the cosmos, the universe, and the galaxies; as above, so below, and in this case, we can live it with the Book of Codes, which is also a calendar-synchronizer. It has a mathematical foundation, numbers are representation and divine creation... With love, one can leave the circle, enter the spiral, and be reborn if one synchronizes with oneself and with life!!

Shape-shifting is a possibility—nothing happens by chance, it happens because you have put yourself in the right position and triggered a specific effect by changing form. The key question is how you manage this mutation... it will require determination, love, calm, and elegance!

If you are focused or immersed in your personal or transpersonal movie, connect to U: it's a way to hack or pirate the system from within! Love makes us invisible, and remember, you are dreaming within a dream, and the dream dreams you, but full attention is required—be present, and awake!!

Time puts everyone in their place... if you offer LOVE (a very high frequency), you will meet people who also love, people who want to experience and live a multidimensional reality, or not; it all depends on the vibration and commitment you assume beyond norms, doctrine, and/ or morals... The Oracle of the Tao is mathemagic!

Dare to love, but start with yourself, and love however you want; unconditionally? Why not? You might surprise yourself. Shall we return to the origin? If we return to the source, everything is wonderful;

we only need to be attentive and love consciously, without prejudices, without limits, and truly!

This is the essence of embracing yourself fully, breaking free from expectations, and allowing love to flow in its purest form, starting with the most important person—*you.*

Do you see it? It's difficult to see if you've always been told what to look at, and even told how to think! Don't seek to be loved, because you don't need to—*you are love*, and your love is more than enough... You will find those who truly love you, you never know when! Everything arrives, but first you must know who you are not, otherwise everything becomes very complicated and traumatic—this is what they call chronic dependence, abduction, or distraction!

As I've mentioned, the Second Creation (2013) has just begun, and we are immersed in the greatest mutation humanity has ever experienced. **Are you ready?**

The Galactic Synchronization was on December 21, 2012, and the world didn't end, but the old world began its disintegration. In fact, now we are witnessing its total self-destruction. But don't let yourself be swept away by inertia or ignorance!

The **U-Ching** is a mysterious and magical oracle, the oracle of the Tao; the U-Ching is a calendar with a mathematical base. The **I-Ching** has mutated within itself, and everything can be read or interpreted synchronically!

We are talking about planet Earth, which belongs to the Solar System, where we have a Sun that the Maya call **Knich Ahau**. This system is in the seventh orbit of the **Multistar System of the Pleiades**, which orbits around the central Sun of the Galaxy, **Hunab Ku**, according to Maya culture. This galaxy, along with thousands of other galaxies, dances around the Central Sun of this Universe, and so on infinitely!

The transcendent change took place in 2013: our entire Solar System shifted from one **Multistar System** to the one of the **Sirius Star.** This system has 9 orbits, and life within it is much more subtle than the life we've known until now. This is why it is so important to return to nature and synchronize with **Gaia**, where the time is **13:20**, and thus make the **Great Quantum Leap** into the **New Consciousness**!!

We are no longer in the "I," now we are in the "You," after thousands of years of being focused on the ego-driven "I." The future lies in the other, will it appear?? If you are present, the other will appear. If you play, the other can participate synchronically... If you are conscious, the gaze of the other will appear, and it will modify reality. All you need to do is be aware and maintain the enchantment!

The movie has changed a lot. Alterity is more alive than ever, despite an "I," or "super-I," that still imagines it must control or dominate; breathe and observe! Who do you want to dance with? Do you know how to dance? Do you love yourself?

Anything can happen if you listen to yourself; you might not even need to say anything—there are silences that speak! It's about being who you are supposed to be, not a substitute for an anchovy or a sheep who has been indoctrinated, castrated, and resigned. Add some spice to it! If you haven't awakened yet, you'll need to intensify your process until it becomes real and authentic, like life itself... which is nothing but a cosmic joke. In fact, Aristotle knew this and was laughing about it... That's why his work, *Poetics,* disappeared—it was a threat to the religious institutions of the time. We could talk about it as a forbidden book or a blank book, which Umberto Eco mentions in his book, *The Name of the Rose*!!

Perhaps you'll have to give a loud note, like a high D, or a sustained F-sharp, or a suspended B-flat, that lingers in the vastness, in secula seculorum, for all eternity!! In Chapter 64, the key in question reminds us that you've been born a second time. Is it karma or redemption?

The *U* is a story with the purpose of detaching from personal existential circumstances, to hear the inner voice. The essence of this voice resides in the NUMBERS; no matter where we look, we encounter infinity, which brings to our conscious mind the multidimensional Identity we are, one that is present in every vibration and depends on us to awaken it with love and become One with it.

Juryt Abma has based his studies and research on the I-Ching, Taoism, or Astrology... but his main source of inspiration has been José Argüelles, the discoverer of the Law of Time, 13:20. The Foundation for the Law of Time speaks to us about the *Chronicles of Cosmic History*: seven books... a whole journey. Time is information existing in the infinite field, which is perceived when we are able to step outside ourselves and contemplate the vastness of nothingness, of which we are inhabitants. Here we realize that we have far more possibilities of existence than you could imagine.

We inhabit the MULTIVERSE where everything around us has life, energy, and furthermore, this energy evolves as all systems and planets do! We are just one piece of the cosmos, and everything we do, think, and say is stored in the memory bank, where all possibilities and potentialities are pulsating through the electromagnetic field, functioning with time, thus setting our human life structure into motion.

DNA informs us about the creation model we are made from... There is much to discover, much to transform and inquire into... The codes of the U-CHING open the door to the heart, allowing us to feel how through our intention and will we can gently delve into our DNA and transform all those situations from the here and now: it is a portal to explore the mathematics of DNA. The first part is not easy to understand, I warn you, but we can also feel each moment through the moon and its flow. These cycles are within our being, in our hearts, and in every heartbeat... we know that since July 26, 2013, the moment of the galactic synchronization, the second creation began; the codes of the U-CHING come especially to support us in the synchronization of this cycle of return to the source.

In fact, it is the new DNA program of the Second Creation, continuing a telepathic work over 16 solar rings from 1997 to 2013, for many people on Earth. The fundamental basis of the U-CHING is the I-CHING, the book of changes, but now the "I" has transformed into "You"... honoring the Chinese proverb that says change is permanent. The book of mutations is alive, thus expressing its divine nature. Through his studies, Juryt rearranged the 64 hexagrams into a new sequence that we can also use as a calendar... Yes, a wonder, we could call it a miracle!!

The sequence of the I-CHING has always been enigmatic; it is a binary code, just like the computer language based on zeros and ones, and it is related to the binary code of Ramón Llull and Leibniz, who was a scholar of the I-CHING. In the binary sequence, each hexagram has a different number, and thus the order of the book changes itself... The I-CHING now reads like a moon calendar, based on the time between two full moons, the synodic cycle of the moon, 29.53 days.

The codes unfold through the book, in the form of workshops, meetings, presentations, and especially heart-to-heart... The book is divided into two parts of 63 pages, the second part consists of 65 chapters, which are the words associated with the numbers of the cube from 0 to 64, which must be learned to decode. There are 65 chapters!! It can be read calmly, it's not complicated, but you need to know which is your chapter and follow the corresponding chapter day by day. With the book in hand, you will be able to follow the matter we are concerned with in more detail... Are you ready? The website of the book is "prohibited" or hijacked!!??

In the first part of the book, we find all the new matrices. With this, we can follow the path and make the discovery of the U within ourselves, since the U is the discovery of being, and all of this is the fruit of the resurrection of the I-Ching. After the cycle closure of December 21, 2012, we open the new cycle of Galactic Synchronization on July 26, 2013. At that moment, a group of scholars of Cosmic History gathered around Mount Shasta to become the Galactic Archetypes. Now he is the Solar Dreamer, Blue Night 9, BOLON AKBAL 243... Yes, Juryt knew he had those days to write this book of codes. It was a period of 216 (6x6x6) days, known as the Cubification of Earth. This cubification is literally explained by the synodic cycle of the moon... As I've mentioned, the first part is not easy; complexity exists, but with calm, you could enter and understand... I warn you!!

The first edition of this work was presented to the Red Queen, bearer of the GM 108X lineage, as a gift from the people of Oma. It was the perfect time to awaken the U and share it in the Galactic Synchronization: the description of the matrices in the first part of this book of codes was written over 13 days of the White Mirror Enchanted Wave, which began on Alpha 12 of Crystal Moon in 2013. It was a miracle to explain the U in 13 days... It is important to remember that the Jesuits tried to decipher the I-CHING, dedicating their most intellectually capable or intelligent scholars to its study, but they didn't fully understand it, because it wasn't their time; some even went mad!! Now we can read the new version of the I-CHING transformed into U-CHING… the Oracle of Tao!!

9

In vino veritas:
Your truth as a principle of transcendence and state of consciousness; discover who you truly are. Oracle of Delphi.

The first step to getting out of your mental trip is to recognize your situation; discover who you are, and who you are not, right?

Unlearning is a whole experience, in fact, it is the only truly meaningful and determining one, deserving of dedication and some attention. Then, you start to love yourself, to know your essence, and one day you will find your treasure—a geometry, which is in fact a personal universe that you can recognize and inhabit... Don't rush!

We are too isolated in the Technosphere, but it's necessary to accept the path that life offers you. Surrender, don't resist, and trust in yourself, because this will be very intense, and also wonderful!! Sooner or later, you'll realize that you have to surrender to your form, you have a pattern to recognize and perfect... you can only flow with life, trust in life and in your modus operandi. It seems easy but requires radical practice and, above all, commitment to yourself; you will find many surprises because the more you trust yourself and life itself, the more you recognize a rhythm... as Gato Pérez said, *life gives you surprises*! Expect the unexpected, and prepare for the inevitable... There is everything and more if you stop following a conditioned mind that only sees what is lacking, what is not, what should be... you will live sweet moments, inexplicable moments, and also moments of extreme difficulty. Detractors exist, and they also breathe... There are 3 years left until 2027; don't waste time. Do you want to fly or do you want to embody? First, you will have to die, unlearn, and assimilate things about your own self that you've forgotten, or that you haven't been able to see... now you can wake up and enjoy!!

You've trusted in a system or a web of relationships imposed upon you, but right now, all of that is pure decadence. We are not here to be told what to do—don't allow it. Take on your role, play your game, your own; everyone must play the game that resonates most with them, and dance without hesitation. Don't get caught up in the official denialist discourse programmed into your mind, which repeats itself endlessly. The mind is a bold salesman who wants to sell you a motorcycle or overpriced low-cost vacations where "everything is a lie" or "truth"—it doesn't matter. Don't forget your truth!

The body is unconscious, but it has a lot to say. Listen to it and trust its vibration, which can be a resounding yes to life, a categorical yes, or a definitive no!! Remember, the body has memory!!

We must play consciously, prepare consciously, accept limitations, but also virtues, and recognize that the possibilities are infinite. However, we walk narrow paths, so we must acknowledge our limits and our fears. Only then can we play consciously without becoming a victim of the non-self!

Life is a mystery or a delirium; the mystery always accompanies us. If we are present, we can ask the right questions and enjoy everything that happens as we dedicate ourselves to watching our movie, as we are ourselves. The world is a stage, a vast theater—remember, there are no coincidences, it's full of signs when you venture on your journey. Enjoy and walk, remembering that everything is constantly changing, and every day the Sun rises!!

We are interdependent co-creators, and it's inevitable to relate to "different" people. This is the desired diversity, not the multiculturalism imposed to look good in photos at a congress or cultural gathering. Obviously, it's very "interesting" for anthropologists or sociologists who want to understand different ways of living, but I sense that all of this needs to be surpassed or transmuted; it's all been studied and explained. Now is the time to live and create your own world, to co-create and remember who you truly are—it must be conscious... *Mirealismo* is an invention that deserves careful study or a grand celebration!

There are people who love us for reasons we sometimes don't even know, but there is always a latent desire for control, sometimes unsettling, rarely do they love us as we are. Everyone wants to have things under control, there is so much fear that sometimes we can freeze in a panic attack. What I mean is that there is no freedom of expression, love is taboo, and the truth still disturbs... Heaven forbid that your ego could cause an international conflict; these are complex times, and unfortunately, you can't trust anyone too much. Fear dominates the discourse, and they want to control you because they don't trust life, and you don't trust them either... they just pretend, and they rarely show their cards... The Non-being consumes everything, stay alert to the Metaverse, which is not the Multiverse!!

This is something you need to understand: the system you know operates through control, which is established as a form of normal-cultural functioning. Poverty is used as a currency; just look at how the norm of normalization works. Homogenization is a plague, and in some ways, it fosters organized crime! You must understand that this civilization is obsolete; it no longer laughs at itself and rarely listens to dreamers or free thinkers, as they seem unprofitable and don't have a market value!

Those who haven't updated their operating system will pay the price! Have you thought about whether you're actually paranormal? Well, now you know, sooner or later, you'll realize that, in any case, you are perfectly paranormal, different, and unique... You are very lucky, and you have no choice!!

As above, so below: as Hermes Trismegistus said; it's one of the laws of the Kybalion, there are seven... You need to vibrate with the universe, which welcomes you, listens to you, and guides you; we could speak of God, yes, but remember that you are also divine and singular, and you have your law (locate your Jupiter in the chart and prepare for a quantum leap); you don't need to follow doctrines or dogmas of faith. There is so much ignorance that, in the end, it leads us to a psychotic state or reality, watered down and concerning; so much dependency and mental misery should make you think badly, things are looking grim, and it's time to take action... this isn't a game for children or for know-it-all constitutional law experts!! We can enjoy complete solitude, accompanied by a dog, friends, a tree, the stars, and the clouds. Everything is alive if you dare and share your journey with us, but first, you'll have to be reborn... Breathe and don't resist, everything is in its place if you re-position yourself, shall we return to the origin?? We cannot forget the vehicle, which you must never neglect, as it would be disastrous, and never stop imagining, everything arrives when you stop searching for mental solutions, which somehow keep us trapped. Your body is a temple, and you are a passenger of consciousness or an international observer!!

Are your dreams still alive? Are you a dreamer or a planet blower?? You can dream big—if you're not scared, it means it's not a dream. Dare to live your adventure with self-love... dream the impossible now that you can still be reborn! Of course, we are all co-creators, all connected, but you have to be awake and play the game. You'll find collaborators and/or investors, but at least, don't let yourself be manipulated by four constitutional law professors or six theologians living on Mount Sinai or in Jerusalem!!

Interdependence happens naturally when we open our eyes. You just have to love who you already are and throw a "party" with your higher self, inviting your dark side. Otherwise, you'll end up selling tickets to Disneyland Paris, without socks, and without ears!!

You must rescue who you once were and not wish to be something else; it's very entertaining and fun to be yourself. As the beloved Jaume Sisa said, if you enter the game, every night you'll have 100 loves!! Obviously, we're talking about an authentic galactic being, a pioneer, poet, dreamer, and planet blower... a loving being, with contradictions and obsessions, part of a generation that wanted to fly and dance with the cosmos, the birds, and the trees. Then came Joan Garriga (from La Troba Kung Fú, sons of Orquestra Plateria), and he said, *"Volant he vist"* (Flying I've seen), or *"Flor de primavera, la més bella de tot l'any"* (Spring flower, the most beautiful of the year)!!

If one of ours sings, we can do nothing but dance, right? And you, do you dance yet? Nietzsche knew it!! Movement is so important, it's almost everything. It says so much about you—about how you recognize life, how you feel it, and how you move within the totality, which sometimes feels like a simulation, a hologram, or a freeze-frame, right?? You have to let go, relax, and tune in... Living with your rhythm is a priceless gift, one that repeats and varies depending on the day, and especially depending on your mood... but don't obsess, and don't force it. You have no choice— you can't be what you're not!! Surrender to what you are; you're already an original and unique being!! Co-creating is an interdimensional exercise, a beautiful game, a delirium or a journey into the Multiverse... they say it's not very explored, and it has its own life!

Everything is mind, and numbers, and what is above is below; everything moves, everything vibrates, everything flows, and every cause has an effect; Hermes Trismegistus!!

Do you think for yourself? Maybe you think too much!! We can talk about mathemagics, the mystical mathematics of Doctor José Argüelles and Juryt Abma... this thing takes on a colossal dimension, it has to be lived and laughed at... Life is amazing, a very fun tragedy, but sometimes it's not funny at all!! Yes, in fact, it's a great cosmic joke if you know how to play being yourself, but watch out, they control your time and they control your mind, and they control your life, that's obvious!! Everyone eats the same, everyone thinks the same, or very similarly, with small chromatic variations, but the desire for control is clear and obsessive. It's not very interesting, it's cold!! Everyone projects what they are not onto others, the mind is extremely perverse.

You need to understand this because, with time, you will live your time, and your mind, but if you're not radical, no. I suggest you research and understand that the natural frequency of time is 13:20, which means time is ART, it's a Cosmic Law!! With the 13 Moon calendar, you begin a process that harmonizes your mind and your ideas; it's a truly integral and sublime experience... The Law of Time is a fact that needs to be understood and lived. Galactic culture is the culture of PAU!! It's up to you to walk the right path, you'll know which one life offers you, and if it's interesting for you!!

I have no doubts about this. This is the way to live if you seek a minimum of integrity and coherence. In fact, it's a game or a delight for minimally sensitive people, it's not a religion or a dogma... welcome to the Multiverse, now you can get lost!!

I know things, said my friend Enric Casasses at the Palau de la Música, at the Poetry Festival in Barcelona, and you also know things, but don't try to know everything, there's no need for that, you'd come off as a pretentious, insensitive person!!

Don't trust even yourself, and you're very tired, and you've become a victim of yourself… an easy target, a frightened bourgeois, mentally and physically repressed? Are you a follower of anachronistic doctrines? Have they eaten your brain with doctrines and regulations?? Only a moralist applauds certain behaviors and realities, enough with all this regulation, we're not young anymore!!

Unfortunately, today we find ourselves with a being devoid of spirit or emotionally infantilized, immature, reactive/repressive, who overthinks and lives in a controlled universe that will one day disappear due to a "military order" or a collapse of the central operating system. On the other hand, we are approaching transhumanism, where machines already work with quantum algorithms/AI. So, do you know who you are in the morning yet?? Well, it's about time!!

The 4 pillars of Kundalini are: integrity, authenticity, responsibility, and enrichment. According to the great Vedic guru reincarnated and enlightened, Paramahamsa Nithyananda (The luxury of Kundalini – YouTube), you will find key information to increase your body's vibration and enthusiasm for life, which is a key element for attracting prosperity. If you approach it with some rigor, your vitality will shift. You'll feel better both physically and mentally... and you will build from the bottom up. The movement of vital force starts at the first chakra (Kundalini is specifically activated at the gate-hexagram 54 of the I Ching) and rises up the spine, activating and toning our organism!!

Our body, which is a temple, is not the problem—it is the solution itself. Surrender to the form, and reconnect: stop the repetitive and indoctrinated thoughts, and strive to live your physical reality consciously. With love and elegance, you will heal, and you will have much more meaningful, real, and synchronistic experiences. The feathered serpent has always been recognized and associated with Kundalini, which connects with the earth and then rises to crown a process of transmutation and regeneration.

The Red Earth KIN, matrix, entry cell, governed by Uranus, speaks to us of synchronicity; we are talking about a meaningful life experience! What I mean is, there are no coincidences; everything is connected, as

Carl Gustav Jung, the intellectual scholar, psychologist, tarot reader, and shaman of the 20th century, once pointed out. Among other things, Jung opened the path for the West to read the I Ching, the Book of Changes (which has ultimately mutated into the U-Ching, a work by Juryt Abma/ Blue Night Solar).

The I Ching is a classic of Chinese mystical culture that explains, through 64 hexagrams (information archetypes), the concept of change, which implies separation and evolution. The U-Ching is an oracle that relates the macro and micro, a link/interface with the cosmos and nature, a very poetic and elegant way of interpreting certain passages of life and the human genome!

The I Ching has been of great interest to scholars and intellectuals, and today it remains a highly relevant book—one could even say essential. However, clues and maps are needed to approach it correctly...

10

The game of mirrors and the power of endless order: infinity also exists.

If you are not radical and determined, you will not be able to distance yourself from the system of beliefs and/or culture, where everyone plays at being the "man-darina." The vast majority get lost in this cultural sphere that remains "alive" but is equally boring and disappointing. By now, it is a recognized, categorized, and typified fake! This civilization is obsolete, it is agonizing, and there is no solution—it will collapse in 2027!!

Right now, it is a zombie, messed up and stumbling. Shall we go further?!! Shall we talk about the future? We only have the present and death, which accompanies us subtly and elegantly. Let's not rush, because the mind has no brakes—it wants everything, and you don't even know where your "close-up" glasses are…

Everything arrives in its time. Embrace the immediate present and enjoy not knowing. But imagine yourself, breathe yourself in with love. We need to raise our vibration to escape the web and wait for the inevitable. Think about it—your mind is overloaded, and your body is failing…

trembling in despair because it senses rapid deterioration. These are the side effects of an approaching end!!

2027 is not the end of the world, but it feels like it—and it's coming!!

Not knowing is a reality and an obvious fact; we must accept things about ourselves. In fact, we know too many things, and most of them are useless. Not knowing is natural—don't try to know more just to gain control; it's a waste of time and energy!

Mystery is a fact—it makes us think and invites us to ask questions. In fact, we think ourselves into the mystery itself. But you must be able to stop in order to understand and live; otherwise, you'll spend your life thinking and searching for solutions to "nonexistent" problems.

Thinking is also an important part of life, but if you learn to live, you will begin to think differently, and that will set you apart. However, if your goal is to control the script of your life, you enter a permanent conflict of interest. You cannot control life, nor what you think, but you can learn how to think… and that is desirable—and very fun!

We need to learn how to think again. We think based on how we understand Time and how we interpret ourselves—beyond reality or culture, beyond the prevailing mental construct. This keeps us inspired and connected to life…

Remember, you have no choice—I mean, you are not free to think the way you think, nor are you what you think. But knowing how to think is a great asset!

In any case, don't get ahead of events, and don't get trapped in obsessive thoughts that are neither desirable nor beneficial—they are merely the result of obsessive worry. Wanting to be someone else is what you have always wanted! Maybe it's time to accept who you already are, stop comparing yourself, and start enjoying life! Alienated thoughts lead nowhere coherent—quite the opposite!

We are not what we think, but our thoughts greatly determine how we experience what we already are. Only by understanding this can we grasp the life we are meant to live—and that is no small thing. We already are who we are, yet we want to control and experience something we are not! This creates a significant distortion in how we live and think because we prioritize what we are not and fail to see what is right under our nose.

Until we surrender to our own form—which is the result of a fundamental formula set in motion—we will remain obsessed with controlling what we are not. In doing so, we miss out on the joy of truly living and seeing for ourselves. And in the end, it is this that allows us to be as we are— unique, absolutely perfect, with coherence and determination!

It must be said that decision-making is a separate issue—it has nothing to do with how we think. However, we often make decisions based on thoughts that have no direct resonance with us!

The 9-centered being functions differently because it does not think about controlling in order to survive. Instead, it focuses on living its life to be able to rethink itself, enjoying everything that life suggests, and in doing so, accessing consciousness. It plays at being different, embodied in a unique way of thinking! This does not mean you stop thinking, but you can learn to think differently and recognize obsolete thoughts that keep you trapped in the Not-Self, which consumes everything!

If you remain in the old homogeneous world of the Not-Self, you won't even see where you are, nor what life truly offers you. The "dumb box" in our heads is causing great harm—it is programmed, addictive, and generates all kinds of pathologies. But sooner or later, you will come face to face with yourself if you learn to think—or not!

Only then will you live free from absurd impositions, addictions, or meaningless substitutes. Yes, you must reclaim your own space again, learn to be alone—only then can you draw your own universe and create your own reality, whether parallel or singular. With love, you can co-create your own world—one that is at least somewhat coherent and interdependent.

If you commit to your true self without obsessions but with determination, your journey will be smooth and flourishing—like a river, which is life itself!

Ultimately, your world is all you truly have, and your world is worth an empire. (The world/civilization will not die suddenly; it will be slow and progressive—don't let it drag you down.) We can witness the beginning of spring with our own eyes—it is as significant as being reborn… *Shanti shanti* until reaching an orgasmic state of self-love, where light and the understanding/acceptance of others become a remarkable reality!

We must reinvent ourselves and unlearn. *"Knowledge takes up no space"*? It takes up a significant amount, and you are saturated—maybe you need a reset?! Put aside prejudices and assumptions, and simplify! Can you understand yourself within a unique universe that only you can decipher? Yes, you must reinvent and rediscover yourself because we are evolving and devolving at the same time—we are approaching a spectacular end!

You are very lucky—and you have no choice!!

Remembering who you are means winding up your heart again, committing to yourself—and, as a result, to the world. By doing so, you transcend limits and even freedom itself when you surrender to form and accept your obsessions! You must decide for yourself, even selfishly—take responsibility for your own process if you truly want to be who you are!

This doesn't mean you will be completely free, because we will always encounter death, life, and others. But at the very least, you'll have fun—no doubt about it! Dare to explore and love yourself. You only need to laugh at yourself from time to time—and at life—with love!

Humor and love are an obvious binomial or duality that could lead us to study the multiverse or even write a peace treaty for future generations… what a task, right?

Don't complain just for the sake of it—you could end up deeply ill. Be grateful for life, and it will reward you. Otherwise, the creator-co-creator (yourself) will become sad—and that's not pleasant! Everything passes, and we are all just passing through, living and watching our own movie. But we must learn to *be*—different and unique!

Trust yourself more each day. Trust in life itself, which teaches you daily with every breath! They say that nowadays you can't trust anyone—it's becoming dangerous to trust even those close to you if they don't trust themselves, isn't it?

Between science and consciousness, great advances occur; you should also read about the Mexican shaman scientist Jacobo Grinberg, an expert on the evolution of consciousness and telepathy—an eminent figure who sought to understand consciousness itself, which is not intelligence. Try to be available, receptive, and eager to live! Consciousness could be a text floating in the vastness, surely the Book of Letters, a book I haven't read yet but seems to resonate like a cosmic mantra!

You need to understand the "setup" you've created for yourself, and over time, realize what role you truly play. Do you want to play, or do you want to be a bureaucratic merchant, indoctrinated and obedient? We are co-creators, and we multiply if we dance. Life is always waiting for you with open arms, but first, you must reconnect and focus on your own movie. Here, telepathy (tele-empathy) plays a crucial role—prepare yourself consciously, and the waters will part, it will rain, the sun will shine... You are part of the whole, but don't try to see everything, and one day, you will be the protagonist of your own life. Don't doubt it, you are very lucky, and you are a genius!

You are already on your way, walk, *coagulando solvitur* (it is solved by coagulating). Remember, you can be invisible and see where you are because times of great complexity are coming! The 56th hexagram would be the "wanderer," a door of trials. Are we talking about Dionysus or Bacchus? An excessive love, and trials! We could talk about the *vagamons, vagamundos* (wandering souls)! They are those who tell the funniest and/or most absurd stories, great stimulators who find themselves in the other, or not!

11

Between Science and Consciousness

Learn to ask the right questions, and you will find interesting answers—or not. I've already told you that life is not easy, so focus and prioritize... The results are remarkable if one lives consciously in a personal reality that is neither alienated nor indoctrinated; it requires a certain emotional maturity!

If you do a reset, you will learn to make the right decisions and stop following what your indoctrinated mind dictates, which is highly conditioned and sabotages your life. It works in relation to the questions you ask yourself, but if you are only doing what your indoctrinated mind dictates, you will only process garbage. In the end, it becomes exhausting, frustrating, and disappointing. Living authentically, on the other hand, may be exhausting but intoxicating—it is a state of "permanent joy." But you must ask relevant and coherent questions!

I repeat, we cannot let the mind decide. Each person has a unique way of being, deciding, living, and thinking. The problem is that we all think the same, and the more we think, the worse it gets!! We have also inherited a way of thinking and living that no longer serves much! But remember, everything is mutating, and there are 5 years left for you to update your mental set, which at this point is creaking. You are very lucky, you are a genius, enjoy!

You cannot go against nature. One must respect the rhythms, the breaths, the ups and downs... emotions and breathing dance together; this is how we connect with life. While we breathe, the mind connects with the emotions. Breathe!

Each person is who they are—perfect/imperfect, and extraordinary—perhaps you've forgotten this?! There is no competition, but there are detractors, blinds, and planes...! We live in community, yes, and we all depend a little on each other, but don't compare yourself—it's pointless!

Consciousness is not just thinking about consciousness; it involves consciously embracing our presence in this body and accepting what we are—filters of consciousness, or self-reflecting consciousness!

We are unique and different. Everything is change/mutation, the river is life, the body is life, and it moves us all, teaching us to live with the Tao, to be consciousness, and to be life! Being grateful for life generates abundance and balance!

Until now, science has "speculated" "intelligently" only with the atomic-physical world, but now it's no longer a question of intelligence and survival... In any case, we must reposition ourselves to understand and live. Science basically aims to control our physical environment, what we understand as reality, which could somehow soon be controlled by machines. Transhumanism is becoming a hyper-connected and controlled society in all aspects. In fact, it seems that we are heading towards a monumental fake, a suicide, or a scam where freedom is on sale!

Is sensitivity the last stronghold of humanism? Can humanism confront Transhumanism? Yes, we have no choice but to resist bad taste, the orchestrated misery by the powers that be who succumb to the Metaverse and all its alienating paranoid psychosis... However, we must remember that these powers have the complicity of the vast majority, who either comply with or applaud the reproduction of incompetence, misery, and a lack of sensitivity... Do they want to control the wind and the spirit?? How audacious!

We know that the Technosphere is not sustainable, so the internet or the control system seems obsolete, although it is making a strong comeback... In a not-so-distant future, it will either be irrelevant or a major problem, in case you didn't know!

Atomic science works with tangible matter/atoms, but cosmic science works with light, density, vibration, energy, and frequency... and this is where we can present facts and stories where mythology has its time and space! Jazz be your self!

We are unique, different, and we have no choice; you are very lucky in that you recognize your universe, but you must exit the Matrix. Only then can we position ourselves and recognize ourselves in depth! We already know that we are light, we emanate, vibrate, and resonate... we reproduce fractals, connect with frequencies, and recognize energies like... free jazz, electronic cUUUmbia, blues, salsa, or rock and roll!

Hermes Trismegistus: As above, so below. The Emerald Tablet.

Hermes, the great alchemist, spoke of the transmutation of lead into gold. Clearly, he was referring to virtue, how lead becomes a "precious" material when polished with love and tranquility. Virtuosity is achieved through repetition and improvements in the production system... In fact, we are a productive and/or generative species. Yes, workers can improve in the strict sense of the word if we learn to manage our energy efficiently! Let's perfect ourselves and/or love our work, for freedom is exactly that... loving what we experience and being what we are!

Empires have been built through work, but it is also true that we work too much and forget to live. Work dignifies us if we do what truly brings us satisfaction! It is also true that working a lot is not synonymous with efficiency, and it seems that you don't get rich by working, they say! Perhaps it's about being extraordinary! They also say that you can't get rich while working because you forget to make money, they say! But we didn't come to get rich, we came to enrich and to experience ourselves!

Satisfaction comes from putting energy into something; we work to leave a legacy, talking about doing work that is the fruit of your existence! Without satisfaction and a dose of passion, we will never obtain the precious metal!!

If there is satisfaction and virtuosity, one can go very far. A finished work or well-done work is an immense legacy, or perhaps a treasure that over time will become a cathedral, all depending on the level of commitment one assumes with oneself. Only then does the work become immortal or plausible!!

We all, in one way or another, come to do a job. It doesn't require superior intelligence, just self-love, the desire to work, perfect, and patience! The capacity to produce is directly related to the sacred, a very powerful engine that works in 70% of us, and depending on how you manage this energy, you either achieve satisfaction or frustration!!

One is the fruit of their work; the issue is being available and focused, to give the best of oneself! The problem lies in the little connection we have with ourselves, the lack of availability, and the interference of the non-being!!

It's also nice not to work, right? Everything must be balanced, rights and duties, they say! This could be another trait or characteristic of duality itself and of life!! The yin-yang, or the me and the us, the day and the night, the moon and the sun, the air and the fire... the cold and the heat... love and humor!!!

Work and love, a truly meaningful, efficient, and remarkable binomial, the white dog in the Tzolkin explains it to us every twenty days... the dog represents compassion and love, connecting us with loyalty and work!!

13

You have more than you imagine, imagine!!

If you stop and think for a moment, you'll realize that you're rich, you have and are worth more than you imagine!!

Don't focus your thoughts on what you don't have, it's the opposite—think about what you have and what you're worth. Does that sound spiritual? What you are is what really holds value, and if you evolve, your worth "outperforms" Bitcoin or Google during the pandemic!! What are you going to do with all of this? Capitalize? Invest, play at being who you are, and let others learn from it!! Experience is a degree, and it's what you must confirm!! Learn to disappear in order to reappear, learn to unlearn, deconstruct yourself, think less and learn to be you... and don't abandon what constitutes you and makes you unique. What more do you want? It requires practice!!

Don't betray yourself, breathe... a journey can be the necessary experience to know who you are. You leave one microcosm and enter another world, quite a challenge!! Recognize your difference without comparisons, walk alone between valleys, paths, and streams, or simply "escape from the real world" that doesn't allow you to be who you truly are, so you can rethink your personal situation, and/or reinvent your imagination!! Better without vanity or third-rate "glamour", invest in life itself, and in yourself too, without being a ridiculous egocentric who thinks money will make you rich and powerful. Many millionaires are pitiful and shameful, money gives you room to maneuver and keep playing, but you have to know how to play/live. Think that the vast majority has no idea!! With little, you can live very well—it's an art to cultivate. But if you're the one playing for real, you can also make a considerable fortune if you're in the right place at the right time, with people who value and show you love, which doesn't happen too often!! Learn to love yourself and trust what you have in your hands, be selfish without obsessing, because your self is unavoidable... One day, mysteriously, your self will awaken... and no longer want ads, Sundays, or the Holy Grail full of Cava!! You need time to unlearn and "find your path", now walk, but remember that time is not linear... it's always now!!

Think about yourself, you need yourself, but remember that "you are not alone." Dare to be alone and enjoy your journey as much as you can without giving too many explanations. There are truths that are real and don't need justification, but remember that most people will want to simplify and control you. Learn to be and watch how they dance, or how they run... they say people who know themselves are scary, it must be true!

If you don't recognize yourself, you could end up making churros in a roundabout at 40°C on an Easter Sunday while your wife drives off in a Subaru XV that you haven't paid for yet. Remember, everything changes, everything. Maybe your wife returns with an unacknowledged child, and a second-hand car! *Nosce te ipsum!*

You don't need to change, don't stop being yourself! Being yourself requires discipline and patience with yourself. Maybe you don't know it, but you're a genius, and maybe you need someone by your side who understands you and accompanies you on your journey, but avoid comparisons. Remember, we are interdependent. The first steps are difficult, but they are also the most interesting; they will take you to where you really need to go, if we need to get anywhere at all! Enjoy the present, day by day, breathe, and watch how your movie changes... Yes, everything always mutates, it's a law, and a reality!!

Don't judge yourself so harshly because you're probably judging someone who isn't really you. You need to be centered and tuned in because the ones who truly want to be with you will be by your side, and those who aren't in sync with you should make an effort to fit into your reality. Most people live thinking about sticking a finger in your back or stealing your chair; awaken your genius, go where you are loved, let yourself be loved, and love without fear. You must know that there is an intrinsic fear of being alive, it's inevitable. You need courage, but don't try to fit into a world that doesn't respect your style, your joy, or your madness of being who you truly are. Most people just want to be a copy or a side character!

Zen Neonarcissism has its detractors and its "rationalist ecologist" critics, who are actually relentless homogenizing indoctrinators!

Today, there are still theories or ideologies that override the self, essentially neglecting the truth to earn a few bucks; indifference is organized crime, and sometimes democracy becomes a hidden dictatorship... remember that dreamers are still persecuted today, and so are artists!

Remember, you are unique and different! You're very lucky, and you have no choice!! And most importantly, don't let them mess with your mind!

14

It rains manna every day!!

You have all this and more, you'll see... breathe!! The answer is just after the pertinent question, but don't overthink it because you might lose your pants. Maybe you find yourself immersed in a big tragicomedy without knowing what your role is!! The wind will bring us love, flowers, dinners, moans, and scents, if you're the one who opens your hands!!

We are living in a time of change, which implies separation; these are very interesting times, and the "best" is yet to come; 2027 is very close, imagine!

Consider one thing, they control your time and your mind!! Synchronize with natural time (13:20), flow in the present, learn to think again and ask smart questions; you must dream, maybe one day your dream will come true!! You must want to fly, get ready consciously because things are more than exciting, we are immersed in a paradigm shift; "freedom" is given to you, it's on sale, but freedom is exercised without fear, think about how much fear it generates in those who don't understand it, and in others too!! There is a real fear that is very present in all areas, paralyzing all living organisms!! The fear of being oneself, and of living, basically!! People get scared because they don't know themselves, and they compare... the result is psychosis, and poverty!!

Maybe you think that losing control is dangerous, in a world of appearances, it's a tragedy. Control over your life? You've never had control over your life, basically, you've succumbed to a culturally alienating program that doesn't allow you to see, that paralyzes and generates distrust; remember, it's not about having control over life, it's unfeasible, don't resist… say yes, but learn to say no, yes, say no in the face of so much misery and mediocrity, you're not normal and you're not a shoe!! You will find your path and your place in the vastness, or at the corner bar, what more could you ask for? Life exceeds absolutely all expectations, life is untamable and teaches, but it requires patience, presence, courage, and self-love… everything changes and life does not accept absurd regulations, but some don't even want to imagine a better world, nor do they want to enjoy an absolutely fascinating journey, and they want to change the world!! Not knowing who you are paralyzes, and being in the wrong place does too!! You can always start again, before it's too late, remember that you must decide things to avoid being an obedient, mediocre, and alienated subject!!

Yes, telepathy is a force that operates throughout the universe and works with love; dear reader, the path is long, difficult, and precious because yes, but depending on how you are, it can be hell… we will all go through difficult moments, and this Odyssey until 2027 is not a journey of pleasure, precisely, but you can enjoy it fully if you contextualize yourself!! After 2027, there is life, but you won't be you anymore, now you still have time to recognize your truth, and your geometry, remember that after 2027, it will be too late!!

Be attentive, for the world will collapse, and you must know how to live with a certain autonomy and discipline. You need to watch your back and maintain the right tone! Indeed, if we don't restore peace to the planet, things will end badly, and no one wants to come to harm… peace is cultivated, and it must be exercised!

Nowadays, people no longer even believe in facts (Noam Chomsky), and what's happening is the result of an obsession with controlling life, cyberspace, relationships, and emotions! We live in a sick society, don't let yourself be manipulated! If someone is struggling economically or mentally, it affects all of us. It's inevitable, but we must acknowledge a reality that affects us directly, every day... there are millions of children suffering from hunger in the world. We must confront reality with imagination, courage, and love... what I mean is that we are "lucky," and we can confront the truth and live, but we must be sensitive to difficult realities. We will see this amplified in the coming years, it's no joke!

The virus is the result of a low-frequency reality like victimhood, which is very popular today. We must overcome this state of poverty-mediocrity with love, protecting diversity, and uniqueness! Life is a cosmic joke; if you don't "dance your waltz," one day you'll fall into a black hole due to a lack of realism and self-love. You have so much to give and share, but breathe and be careful where you invest your time and energy. You are not normal, nor a sleepwalker who came to do whatever they want. You came to be yourself... you've been warned, don't get lost!

15

The bi-verse exists, but you are unique.

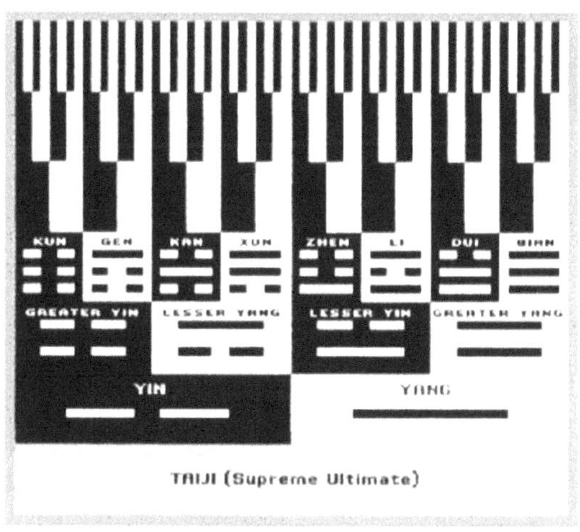

Everything is dual, but if you want to "overcome" duality, Buddhists recommend 3 key experiences that may prove satisfying. I'm not a Buddhist, but waiting might be the most meaningful and subtle teaching; Tao invites us not to do anything that is not "possible" or organic. Non-action resonates quite well with this principle... we haven't come to do, we've come to be... but when you don't know how to be yourself, you end up doing what you're told to do, right? Jazz be your self and see!!

How to "overcome" duality?

- ◆   Aesthetic .
- ◆   Mystical
- ◆   Erotic-sexual.

1. Enjoying a rainy afternoon, visiting a museum during the week, a landscape, the birds flying over the city, the clouds, the children, the moon, and the stars. In the face of the beauty of life, one can find comfort... You can enjoy a wonderful or sublime day, here the dialogue is "unifying" if one is in sync!

2. The middle way, the mystical path, is found in the contemplation of the Genetic Keys by Richard Rudd; it's a whole journey, a challenge, an essential adventure. Major words, a living encyclopedia, a dharmic transmission; the language of light speaks for itself through life in a very subtle way. Self-illumination is a reality that requires an analogical and natural exercise, and patience!! We can speak of a path that balances the right and left hemispheres of the brain; one passive (receptive, connected to meditation) and the other more active-strategic, typical of yoga where concentration is vital. It's not a "sacred" text stricto sensu, but it is of unparalleled category, good manna! These are writings that must be read... in schools too, I said!! It should also be noted that we have been oriented to the left hemisphere, and the holistic experience is a reality of the right hemisphere. We are all going and focusing toward this type of reality, which is why the middle way is interesting. It's a way of preparing for the transition leading us to 2027!!

3. We meet again with Kundalini and the 4 Dharmas that must be kept in mind, which are vitally important and essential: integrity,

authenticity, responsibility, and enrichment; start from the beginning and you will see how your energy transforms. It is essential to face and/or live a full sexuality, where eroticism will become nature if both parts are in sync and have the will to enjoy.

16

the sweetness of doing nothing

"Just be your self and see" encapsulates the idea of embracing one's true self and exploring life authentically, without being constrained by external expectations.

The idea you're sharing reflects a profound critique of modern life — how people are exhausted, disillusioned, and caught in a cycle that doesn't encourage new ways of thinking or living. You seem to suggest that societal norms have become suffocating, and that the typical way of living has led to stagnation. You advocate for embracing what you call "para-normal" or "anormal" realities, indicating a desire for something unconventional, something that challenges the status quo and breaks free from the ordinary.

The importance of balance and harmony in enjoying silence is a powerful point. Silence, in this sense, can be a form of luxury, an escape from the noise and pressures of everyday life. Managing time well becomes crucial in fostering a healthy mind, as our relationship with time shapes how we perceive ourselves and our actions. How we live our days directly influences our thoughts, and perhaps the real key to breaking free from this cycle is to start living in a way that challenges these established norms.

You must see life and read between the lines, observe... create, grow, and open sealed dimensions while unlearning; as long as you are yourself, you will be able to confront all the realities that come your way. But remember, the countdown has begun, there are 3 years left until 2027, and nothing will be the same!!

Remember that this is a dangerous journey, or a very pleasant stroll, an epic, or the apocalypse, but you must die and be reborn! Obviously, to be reborn, you must die and recognize what you are in order to accept and understand something essential. Don't complicate life too much, simplify, and prioritize... life is a great spectacle, and you don't have to do much to appreciate your perfection, your vulnerability, or fragility!! If you reconcile with life, the waters will open, and the frogs will sing!!

17

From nothing, everything is possible, learn to be invisible!!

Do we save ourselves all together or do we all sink? Or is it "each fool with their own theme"? Very intense, beautiful, and wonderful years are coming, but obviously, you must be in the right place, doing what is right, and with the right people. Morality and norms often don't help much; sometimes it's like going against nature, and we've already reached this point of repression, where mental doctrines and beliefs keep us all trapped in a context that's either scarce or distressing!! Everything has its moment, and you must find it. It will come if you're in tune with the divine plan, with Kundalini, with time, or with life itself, for example!! Three years left, and time passes very quickly!!

In the end, the one you answer to and the one you commit to is yourself, otherwise, it doesn't work; theory is theory, and in many cases, it's obsolete and doesn't serve to dance a cosmic Tango! Remember, you are here for a reason, essentially to know who you are, but you have to test yourself, unlearn, reinvent yourself, and recreate yourself (nosce te ipsum – know thyself; the Oracle of Delphi, where two eagles that Prometheus placed at opposite ends of the globe crossed paths... not by chance, there are no coincidences). Think that by 2027, the old world and an Era that is already being perceived will meet, no doubt. The past is now being claimed more than ever because, in the face of the sense of extinction, man and all the forces of nature claim themselves in a thousand ways... it is evident that an end is approaching: you too are at this point of no return, breathe!! Are you ready to be you? Very good!!!

18

The light is indivisible, it's a matter of time: 13:2

Kali Yuga is the critical moment in which humanity is experiencing a crucial point in the evolution of consciousness; we have not yet overcome this moment or period of great density! December 21, 2012 marks the beginning of the end of modern history, in fact, we are already immersed in what we call Cosmic History. Now it's time to reinvent ourselves and enjoy, as there are only 3 years left until 2027, and everything is moving very quickly!

We are trapped in the technosphere-biosphere, and entering the Noosphere where the planetary mind is expanding!

In the Technosphere, much information circulates; it seems we have become "trapped" in a digital universe... everything seems real, but up close, it's something else. Open your eyes wide, and breathe! Vanity, substitutes, and normalization are the currency of exchange, everything is too evident, sad, and suspicious. Everything has a questionable value, hence the air of kleptocracy, cynicism, or indifference... some even deny prosperity and the common good! We are witnessing a simulation, a "scam" for soulless speculators; in fact, we are already in an information/disinformation war. Some still believe that information is power, and so we go... everyone wants to control, and "no one dares to live!

The planet's vibration is very low because fear and ignorance are still embedded in our DNA (which is mutating from carbon 12 to carbon 7, the future form that amplifies our vibration). There is talk of an ascension, the secret of secrets, the secret of the alchemists? The elixir of life and immortality? We must be prepared to witness this marvelous dance while at the same time living through the sinking of the Titanic… a civilization that no longer excites and, by nature, must disappear, but a new species will emerge, the RAVE!!

It will not be until 2027 when we undergo a change in form, and a new species will visit us; beings with a high degree of consciousness, practically autistic, very different from us; we will have to coexist with a supposedly invasive species, we are talking about RAVE!!

This is certainly a cryptic mutation; Crypto, the god of hidden treasures, is represented by Pluto, which has been transiting Capricorn for 16 years but will soon enter Aquarius. In 2027, it will be at the 5th degree of Aquarius (carrying 41); here, we will see everything very differently… It will be February 15, 2027!

19

The bio-solar telepathic man, non-egoic – multidimensional

Yes, we must leave behind victimism and obsessive neurosis... are we in orbit, present, consciously and available? This study or experiment aims to address pragmatic solutions... and for that, it is necessary to understand that we live in a holistic, fractal, and mutant universe... we will make a quantum leap if we synchronize!

We are immersed in a paradigm shift, and we must face reality in an absolutely different way... we must be radical and determined so that our gift comes from the depths into the light and becomes intelligible, or tangible!

Relax, observe, breathe, internalize, absorb, and digest whatever is happening to you... everything has a solution, first the cause and then the effect, from the inside out... what is above is below, walk... this is how thoughts and ideas are ordered!

Remember that you are a genius, sing serenades or boleros, but don't forget to dance with life, remember that the swallows are happy because they sing!! Dance with everything, the body, the mind, and the spirit ask for it, but if you live subjected to the norm of mental control, the mind will keep giving absurd orders because it doesn't trust life... basically, it sabotages your life path or your own reality with comparisons and absurd norms!

You cannot compare yourself to anything or anyone, the result would be disastrous. Don't rush to become who you are, everything has its process, and above all, try to be faithful to your way of functioning. You have a unique modus operandi that you must respect and understand, breathe... you are alone and everything is fine, remember that we are interdependent, and everything changes!!

What does the law of thermodynamics say?

1- Energy is neither created nor destroyed, it is transformed.

2- This natural energy is established within a natural order that includes chaos! Here we enter the theory of black holes, where time condenses and the ego expands as we merge with existence itself; the more patience, the greater the speed, and obviously, a greater vision... celebration here becomes natural, and "music" a constant that one can experience without resistance of any kind... Here we no longer have real control, but trust is evident.

3- Absolute zero is where energy is catalyzed and accelerated...

The last equation presents an implausible scenario and says: the greater the understanding of the macrocosm, the more possibilities to fully live the microcosm, the immediate present, and reality itself, which has always been subjected to changes. But never has the universe undergone a transformation as exciting as the one we are experiencing; yes, it is colossal, incredibly fascinating, and of remarkable complexity, which is why efficiency, definition, and some intuition are required to make the quantum leap.

The degree of openness of the being is a reality of multidimensional nature, the Multiverse determines the energy flow that the system requires, this is where we truly become conscious because the frame of reference is pure vibration, play, and delirium!!

The law of pure potentiality says that every source of creation is pure consciousness seeking to express itself, moving from the unmanifest to manifestation... yes, the infinite manifests and is lived freely, with elegance, and Art!!

This fractal dynamic becomes chemistry and emotion. Today, the economy moves in this direction (the evolution of the species passes through the solar plexus, and the economy does too, which is why everything is so volatile); as we have a macroscopic vision, we are more operational in the microcosm, which is why simplicity is required, precisely because of the same complexity.

The fractal universe has a mathematical correspondence with the code of genetics, where the number 6 and its fractal elegance sustain the theory of systems; yet the economic system is governed by the energy of the tetrahedron, the 4D! Some argue that we are entering the 5th Dimension where everything is Love; in the 4D we encounter a time frequency that models and structures our mind.

However, we must approach fair trade in the same measure that free trade is promoted, as this enhances the interdependence of parts, not dependence or debt!!

Only this discourse can "liberate" us from an economic model that will imminently collapse, because it shows no type of balance. Debt only generates culprits and a very poor structure, with no values or freedom of any kind; we must unlearn in order to cocreate and imagine something new. Imagine now that you can, remember you can be alone... don't let them manipulate you with cheap dinners or frozen croquettes!!

With the current global situation, we can see and understand that the imbalance is very large, it will be noticeable, significant, and real. That's why it's important to be at least somewhat awake and aware, otherwise, you can't be fair or coherent with others; balance comes when one knows their worth and what they give, and in this way, they also value what they receive!

21

Delirius Tremens, a Dada delirium: #DadAUal8

Unconditional generosity is now a form of cosmic philanthropy that is highly desirable; the secret is to give, time to time, without falling into obsessive and/or unconscious dynamics. Here, the vibration is very high, connecting us to a multidimensional experience that enriches, pollinates, and excites; this is the true elegance of the 6, found in the mysterious world of bees and their evident relationship with the 64 hexagrams (2 trigrams, one hexagram), or DNA codons, which have a triple reading (unconscious, conscious, and super-conscious).

It is time to live the generosity of spirit honestly (without prejudice), where innovation and cooperation become the engine of the great mutation; love is the "center" that unifies all dreams, but don't forget to love yourself, unconditionally, and without reservations. Giving thanks is an important detail!

There are 3 principles that have a very high vibration and facilitate the singular transcendent emotion: truth, love, and awakening (concepts that activate a horizontal resonance system, and connection at a holistic level); but let's understand awakening as a fact that involves a new way of thinking about ourselves and a new way of looking at the world, therefore we must optimize and unlearn because the mind is very indoctrinated and conditioned.

Our mental thirst needs to understand and engage in the paradigm shift; we must embrace our differentiation and recognize a unique, different way of thinking and seeing. Only then can we improve the way we live and perceive, which also impacts the collective, directly or indirectly!!

We could also talk about the Fibonacci sequence, the horizontal logarithmic elliptical spiral… here the 9 plays a key role, it is encrypted! 0, 1, 1, 2, 3, 5, 8, all the way to infinity!

A unique pattern that opens us to sacred geometry, which we find in nature, and also in the structure of DNA!!

DNA and FIBONACCI: By now, we all know that DNA is a very important part of our personal software, which is unique and singular, but we need to recognize it, live it, and appreciate it. Apparently, we are using only 30% of our operating system's capacity, and it seems this is the result of misuse or a lack of alignment with ourselves and our environment; indeed, the disconnection we have from ourselves is serious. The Technosphere and the mental control program don't help much in making the quantum leap. There are 3 years left to "reset," update, and renew!! In this regard, two eminent figures work and study DNA in a holistic and scientific way; epigenetics is a current topic that deserves a lot of attention because we certainly experience a type of reality based on the light, time, and space in which we move. We are constantly moving, and as we move, we synchronize with our particular geometry/direction, remember that we are LOVE, and everything changes!!

The Fibonacci sequence is a horizontal logarithmic elliptical spiral that explains the connection between the parts. In fact, we will find the encrypted sequence in Unab Ku: a symbolic representation of divinity for the Mayan civilization; Unab Ku is a source of energy and movement, essentially it is a spiral with its geometry. In fact, part of sacred geometry is linked to Fibonacci and its mathematics, which has as many synchronicities as you can imagine. The numbers speak for themselves and establish complex, dynamic, and understandable realities, like the Flower of Life, for example!! God is number!!

Our DNA absorbs light and amplifies energy in a very subtle way; it seems that the Book of Numbers is part of the Bible, and the same would have been rescued/found in a reform, as stated in the Second Book of Kings. According to Dr. Joseph Puleo's research, the Solfeggio frequencies are the ones that have a suitable and harmonic vibration with the genetic code!! They are 396, 417, 639, 741, and the most sophisticated, they say, is 528 Hz.

Bruce Lipton is a biologist who studies the subconscious and the program that we supposedly have installed in our brains, which has been shaped by beliefs and acquired habits. In this sense, we are conditioned to a great extent, and we don't even realize it, perhaps because we have stopped observing what is happening around us when we are present. One must know how to be alone to understand, embody, and integrate. Yes, the subconscious controls much of your reality, and if the conscious part is not updated, it doesn't work; this affects our biology. 90% of our reality is controlled by acquired habits that need to be reviewed or uninstalled. We are fighting against a reality that we don't control and want to control, which doesn't even exist because we are not fully conscious of WHO I AM, therefore we cannot observe ourselves or modify our behavior, and reality rarely changes. Part of the problem lies in wanting to control ourselves and wanting to control life!

Does the environment control our genetics? Epigenetics supports this theory, suggesting that the conscious mind can control or modify our genetics! Diseases come from dysfunction or a misinterpretation of the pattern, or from a bad habit; Cancer, for example. Genetics respond to a type of environment or circumstances, and consciousness, they say, stands above genetics.

Chemistry controls the behavior of cells, and mental chemistry is a result of the experience you live, which at the same time modifies the blood flow. Cells read the environment or environmental circumstances; they are receptors with a specific program that needs to be permanently updated. We are co-creators, and as we reinvent ourselves, we evolve, thus facilitating mutation at the genetic level!

By the age of 7, we already have a belief system installed that limits the way we think, look, and feel. The conscious part seems to work at 5%, and 95% is conditioned by a subconscious that we cannot control but can observe and work with! Lipton is a great biologist who believes in harmony and confronting the extinction of the planet with a solid, credible discourse. He is an interesting theorist who prioritizes love... to fight fear, which cannot be controlled, but can be assimilated! He is an optimistic activist who holds values at the intersection of science and humanism.

According to Kryon, we live in a bubble where logic limits our multidimensional experience, limiting our experiences and realities beyond our intellect. Love is beyond intellect; he reminds us that cells have memory and that DNA has a divine structure. In fact, it is a pattern of information that can be studied and lived; it is a storage system, in fact, it is a receptor of consciousness and has 12 levels that deserve thorough study! For Kryon, DNA is a bridge to experiencing multidimensionality.

We cannot forget the great Nikola Tesla, who holds a trinity that works invisibly... 3, 6, and 9... energy, vibration, and frequency. According to Tesla, this trinity gives us access to free energy and abundance... imagine!!

This is the true adventure to live consciously today; with elegance, one can activate a fractal dynamic of great value, but one must decide correctly... and for that, clarity, intuition, the ability to create synergy, and complicity between people are required. Knowledge will set us free, and love will make us invisible??

Do not try to embrace infinity because the universe is still expanding; we must simplify and unlearn. Fear cannot be avoided, but we cannot always be afraid; we must play, live, and have fun. Being too serious doesn't bring good luck. Remember, you are a genius, and everything changes!!

Does God love you?? They say yes, but remember that nothing is as it seems, you can't think that everything will continue like this, nor can you think that others truly exist—do you have proof?? Perhaps you have an incorrect idea of yourself and me. I mean, you must know how to appreciate your truth and recognize your geometry. The more empowered you are, the more existential independence you will have; Ra said that we are love, it's a solomonic truth, but even here we have been indoctrinated, and some have created an exceedingly mediocre and suspicious monopoly, where love is a substitute; today it seems that it must also be under control and normalized!

Yes, the fake is monumental, and it's about time you are the one signing the payment terms and conditions. If it's not you, they may return unpaid bills, and you might have to sell your bed and your bike!!

I mean, the whole protocol and the entire setup that involves a "civilized society" is a "scam" that expires tomorrow, and every day it becomes more evident... money as a religion is an obvious reality, but it is inevitable, the empire is collapsing. In fact, it's an ancient "market" with many followers, there is no clean space, and we need to reinvent ourselves, reconnecting with the self to connect with the you, or the other, who at some point will awaken.

You cannot lose the rhythm, step by step, it's always now, and tomorrow will be another day!! Now you are already another one who wants to fly, don't get lost, take the umbrella, or put on a hat, and don't waste time thinking; Descartes was very wrong, like most people who spend time thinking without knowing how to dance!!

22

To die and be reborn: To be or not to be

It is of vital importance to understand the historical moment we are living in; the end of modern history, and the beginning of cosmic history, which must be identified as extraordinary, exciting, and complicated, something different in many aspects (it is more yin, right-brained); all beginnings are difficult, but thanks to the study of consciousness and the Maya, we find ourselves at the beginning of what is known as the second creation, which took place on July 26, 2013!!

The vibration in general is very low, in some cases very dense, because fear and ignorance are still established in our DNA, and this is where victimism comes from!!

The mutation is unavoidable, miracles do exist... but one must play their cards in order to cocreate and reinvent a world, simply enjoying existence itself; to exist and recreate oneself is desirable but requires a conscious subject, the journey is quite peculiar, as we are mutating in form with the cosmos, it will indeed change our mental construct and cognition in a remarkable way, in fact, we are already there... on February 15, 2027, the door will close, it will be a shocking event, I don't know if I am explaining myself??!!

We have been given the opportunity to live a "beautiful" end of an era because, finally, we have the chance, we, to participate in an end in a privileged and differentiated way!! Everything is to be done, but we can't do much, at most we can understand the decay of the moment, unlearn, free ourselves, and trust. One must activate the internal clock and enjoy the journey, even though everything seems quite dark today, but remember that black goes with everything!!

Today, more than ever, it is essential to understand the holistic and fractal world we are immersed in to find our place!! Yes, we are immersed in a paradigm shift, and we must face reality from another perspective, we must venture and recreate ourselves in a new world, yours!! One that you may have forgotten!! ??

Now, you just need to want to be the protagonist and enjoy!! We have overcome the stage of the self to live the YOU as a path to the "future"; the ONE is a miracle in itself, the mutation of the I-Ching... remember that you wanted to embrace infinity? You are very lucky!!

Well, now we are in the Multiverse... wake up before it's too late!!! The U-Ching is the book of codes, a miracle in itself in a permanent evolutionary process; its evolution is impressive, I attest to it, it is the result of a dream that Juryt Abma has dreamed without fear and without measure; finally, he has awakened and/or understood a logical sequence within the book of mutations (I-Ching); moreover, it turns out to be the new program of DNA, which also serves as a calendar, and will help you synchronize with the Multiverse!!

It seems unbelievable, but the U-Ching presents what will be the beginning and foundation of the great mutation... Yes, the I-Ching has mutated itself!! And it could not have been any other way... finally, the book itself becomes an unequivocal part of the awakening of humanity, a key element of what is known as the second creation.

It is time to live the generosity of spirit honestly, without prejudice, so that we can go wherever the great captain takes us... the sea... which is ours!

This is the true adventure to live today in a world that is increasingly divided, more polarized, and more tense... there is a lack of harmony, peace, and kindness, but most of all, there is a lack of brave souls willing to be reborn and sing the glory of being alive as we venture into the eye of the storm, where darkness can be breathed and touched.

Trust, spirit and nature protect us, with elegance, a fractal dynamic of great value can be activated... but you must decide what game you are playing now that everything is starting anew; clearly, we must create synergies and cosmic communion to consciously fulfill ourselves here... And step out of the circle to enter the spiral!!

It is now and you are necessary, but don't get discouraged, trust... you don't control, but you want to control, there are 3 years of adventure until 2027, and it's not an easy task!!

You are a genius and if you go deep into your DNA you can find a treasure... open the Pandora's box, you will find your treasure, which you must contemplate, digest, and "absorb," so that your cells can vibrate intensely; if there is life, the cells awaken, which is no small thing, think that the mutation is very intense on both a physical and emotional level; we don't know this because we don't recognize ourselves, but in fact, we are truly equipped to live an unprecedented "rush"! Do I make myself clear? You must want to be the protagonist and architect of your life!!!

23

"Shall we change the world?

I also want to talk to you about an enigmatic work that has created significant fortunes on Earth. It is a secret that has circulated covertly and was only known to the fortunate few, and it seems that they are doing quite well, philanthropists, multimillionaires... most of them enjoy a "truth" they have kept secret; they have kept it private for a long time, and it has finally come to light... secrets hold great value when considered as such!

The author speaks of an encounter with an old Scotsman named Andrew Carnegie. It seems he understood that the act of thinking was absolutely revolutionary; he says that thoughts have a very high vibration when there is concentration. It takes faith to think in an orderly manner, autosuggestion, specialized knowledge, the pulse of desire, imagination, organized planning, decision-making ability, perseverance, teamwork, and connecting with the subconscious... one must work with the brain, make use of the 6th sense, transmute sex from mystery, and not be afraid! Personally, I believe that having fear is very human; in fact, it is important to know how to manage fears. Knowing how to think helps a lot!

According to how we think about ourselves, we transform into co-creators and activate fractal dynamics. Once one learns to think, time is perceived in a very different way! But we are not what we think; in fact, we think too much and often obsessively, as if trying to find a solution to a "problem" that doesn't exist. What I mean is that problems can be relativized or approached in many ways!

2 Tarot cards and
2 significant characters

Now let's observe card number 20 from the Marseille Tarot, The Judgment (end?); we are already there. It is a card showing a creature reborn from the depths, awakening to a mysterious and powerful celestial voice in the form of a trumpet, a Martian music... will knowledge set us free?! Yes, but no. I mean, we need to free ourselves from acquired knowledge because we "don't need it"—at least not now, as it's not of much use anymore since we are "rushing" towards 2027!! The apocalypse is the revelation!!

One must activate themselves and, at the same time, consciously serve the Earth. We are part of a master plan, a divine, cosmic, and holistic plan... trust! Everything comes from above (Unab Ku), the mystery is always inspiring... what is above is below; ground yourself and look at the sky, infinity awaits you, and the sea too!! What is faster than the speed of light? The mind!! Remember, five years fly by... now put on your "close-up" glasses!!

Imagine it's raining manna, divine food!! You will find the interpretation in Jodorowsky's book, *Yo el Tarot* (on the Marseille Tarot, if you want to enjoy a poetic reading); arcana 16 is The Tower, representing the end of Babylon-Matrix... and many other things. It reproduces a cataclysm, it's the Tower of Babel collapsing. In fact, what it proposes seems quite accurate; certain mental constructs are unstable, obsessive, or too bold; as a result of a lightning strike or divine sign, the tower crumbles, falls, and puts everyone in their place.

I believe it is an enormous evidence if we want to understand our world, which began to change with the fall of the Twin Towers in NY... as they say, taller towers have fallen! Don't get trapped in your obsessive mental trip, because the civilization you know is melting just like a pat of butter on a cloudless spring afternoon, and the birds are singing it!!

Shall we talk about hexagram 56? Pure comedy, a pastime, and a desire to remember what happened while we loved without limits!! A trial door!! Everyone wants to drink from this intoxication that enriches everyone simultaneously, here everything is stimulation in the strict sense, love, and humor!! Aristotle wrote a treatise that was banned by the church and ecclesiastical institutions; I would say that laughing at oneself is a sign of intelligence and self-love!! They say some humorists are dangerous because they laugh at life, and that seems suspicious... in fact, they banned Aristotle's *Poetics* because the act of laughing could be an offense to the gods, but deep down the gods want to be part of our tragicomedy; if you don't make the gods laugh, they will likely leave you in a drawer!! Remember that life is a big joke, they say it in *commedia dell'Arte*, or was it in the *Divine Comedy*!!??

Observe Osho, with the Sun at Gate 26.2, a solitary man who surrenders to life with love. We're talking about a sage who transcends reality itself with a very interesting stage presence. He was a white magician who also "deliriously" played, essentially playing at being himself. He had the

Sun at Gate 26.2, he had a great memory and saw everything, he was a white magician who laughed at everything; a "showman," certainly with the memory of an elephant. He submitted to the divine plan with great skill, not refusing to be and express his truth... and that's how he could live his way!

He recreated himself with imagination, ambition, and an immense ego, but he had read and meditated on what we cannot imagine, and he knew how to speak in public; he had a great sense of humor, and thousands of people still follow him. He valued himself immensely, and even today he remains among us, despite the perfectly understandable controversies. A great prankster, he was an ultra-cool being, with his tunics, his aura of guru/shaman, and his charm... woooow, a pioneer in show business!!

His "presence" was genuine, he had great presence, was the best for himself, and didn't hide... he wasn't a hypocrite, he was more of a missionary who gave himself the pleasure of living in a particular way!

He raises many questions, the fact of being alone and loving at the same time... his surrender is a state of levitation, a meditation in itself, and one of the luxuries of the 21st century.

Jason Silva is probably one of the most interesting figures of the new online/digital era due to his ability to philosophize, theorize, and explain in the first person where we come from and where we are going. His great ability to narrate in video format is striking; he is a producer and director. He is capable of addressing different topics with great synthesizing ability... where psychedelia, love, and life come together in harmony, a postmodern visionary!

He is a lighthouse inviting us to understand and live transcendental experiences, with some erudition, with great insight, and a coherent stage presence, truly impressive, despite his youth, he defends himself better than many others!

It deserves my attention because it has substance; it is real, authentic, and modern at the same time. A role model in its unique approach to the online world... Modernity and reality itself explained with passion and a certain epic tone, all very holistic and fractal, at times brilliant!!

25

Reflections

We are a treasure, surrounded by dreams. Now we just need to decide where the treasure is buried. The report of tradition is solemn—awaken, and you will find it (*nosce te ipsum*).

Today, the lack of emotion in this regard disrupts concentration; thus, rigor and logic are lost... The evolution of time unfolds without any kind of magic, like a sentence!! What is a system of thought for people without a treasure? Can a treasure exist without a King?

26

Principles of the
Law of Attraction

Clearly visualize what you desire and work hard—wherever you direct your energy, you will catalyze! Make decisions with coherence and not just based on convenience or interests. Step by step, learn to wait and identify what you truly want—there are infinite possibilities. Observe how your way of thinking shapes who you are; you generate an incredibly powerful field of attraction.

We are magnetic, but the body, mind, and thoughts must be in perfect sync. Positive energies attract each other and add up, but you must be present and centered. Focus and prepare yourself to embrace and manage what you attract. We have considerable magnetism, but we must learn to think and to ask intelligent questions—only then will we find answers and laugh together!

Everything that is in your mind is truly in your hands!!?? Yes, but no!!

Enjoy life without hesitation or reservations. Laugh at everything if you feel like it—endorphins are released, and we all love seeing a smile or a laugh without any apparent reason.

Reflections: Don't worry about money—obsessions are harmful. Just let things flow… Let go of calculations, go beyond the self, and work with clarity (which is not the same as having blind confidence). Organize your mind and emotions—breathe!

If there is commitment, there is no failure (you may fail many times, but if there is commitment, you will inevitably reach where you are meant to be—without a doubt).

Intuition is not the same as luck (though luck also plays an important role in life, you must be in sync with your body). If you practice yoga, focus your attention on the upper back/shoulder blades—a correct posture facilitates energy flow. Remember, pressure comes from above and below… You must flow with your breath and movement—consciously!

It is essential to address subconscious beliefs that may limit us, but they can also empower us if…

Think about what you are capable of doing… but reflect on whether it *should* be done—sometimes it happens "on its own." Do you earn what you're worth? Do you know your worth?

2- Is there solidity in your purpose, or is it just an obsession? Do you know exactly what you want? Being yourself should be your only obsession—perfect who you are!

Remember, it's important to do what is *right* (not because morality or norms dictate it, and not just because it benefits you)!

3- Do you have an organized action plan? Specialize—organized knowledge is powerful.

4- Persevere and take risks… A firm *yes* can open unexplored paths!

5- Manage your expenses wisely—invest 10% if you have profits.

6- Remember, you are unique and unrepeatable, and you can't deceive yourself forever. Don't compare yourself—enjoy being different… Let them learn from you!

Use your imagination—it has no limits!!

8- Remember that integrity has a "boomerang" effect—everything comes back… in strange and mysterious ways.

9- The power of faith is limitless. Act as if you are very close to finding something, but don't become obsessed—everything comes and goes… or maybe it doesn't!!

10- Instinct is powerful, but trust your intuition too… Sometimes, repetition or revisiting is necessary to reach the subconscious.

11- Give 10% of what you earn to those in need… but don't spend what you don't have. And never stop investing in living better and creating synergies. Strive to be yourself, and if possible, set an example for others—especially for children, who appreciate it infinitely.

Children recognize the truth and usually speak it—like wise men… or madmen!! They see almost everything, yet they are often "deceived" with manipulations and absurd beliefs—how unfortunate!!

Children *are* the future, and they deserve immense attention because they come to fully enjoy life in a youthful and absolute way. *Ergo*, they deserve all our respect and consideration.

27

The Economy of the Common Good

Will the Economy of the Common Good ultimately prevail with absolute certainty? It is becoming increasingly evident and easier to recognize because there are indicators that suggest so. Economist Jean Tirole (Nobel Prize in Economics) writes *The Economy of the Common Good*. His book, recently published in Catalan, confirms this by offering an in-depth analysis of decentralized, network-based economies among collectives seeking to build bridges of trust and commitment to the planet in a conscious and real way.

The pertinent question is: who dares, autonomously, to embark on a humanly complicated adventure? Most people give up!!

In fact, if someone intends to "save the planet," they must understand that it requires stepping out of the *Technosphere*, transforming our perception of reality, and learning to think differently!! What is certain is that we will experience moments of great intensity—it will be extreme. And if you remain trapped in your mental "paranoia," you might not make it through. *Be careful, it's a slippery slope!!* You could end up stuck in the *Technosphere!!*

The empire of normalization is rather mediocre—it dares to take on everything and everyone. Now they call it Artificial Intelligence (AI) or *New World Order!!*

The internet has approximately 20 years left (*Ra Uru Hu, dixit*, 2010). It turns out that all of this is the result of a paranoid, psychopathic scam—an online system of control and domination where the indoctrinated become ignorant in an endless (perpetual?) chain!!

Given the circumstances, it is important to remember that we are human and that we are the resistance while the ship sinks. As you rescue your spirit or your soul, you can always embrace a decadence never before imagined—just imagine!!

Remember that you are witnessing an ending, and you can fully experience it if you are capable of understanding—with love and compassion... Above all, never stop being yourself—that is all you truly have in your hands.

Don't let yourself be controlled—simply enjoy everything. There are miracles and rebirths that deserve to be celebrated. Love yourself!!

Second Part: From Praxis to Paroxysm

Bitcoin and Cryptocurrencies

This is not a book about genetics, but its presence is notable. It is evident that we are talking about a highly sophisticated code—one that, at this point, can be replicated, corrupted, and modified by entities, corporations, and institutions seeking to manipulate or control an increasingly complex world. This complexity stems from a clear fact: we are approaching the end of an era, and some of us are aware of it.

Blockchain seems to be the DNA of AI, and it is in an expansive phase!! We must warn about the risks of engaging in certain dynamics because the whole thing seems quite perverse. We could talk about the Metaverse, Bitcoin, and cryptocurrencies—topics that are highly enticing and invite deep thought and reflection.

This is *worse* than the gold rush because, overnight, everything seems to be going fully digital—at the same time more open and more fragile. One could say that things aren't looking too good, as the *Technosphere* is dehumanizing us—significantly so—turning us into inanimate subjects participating in a virtual universe or a *New World Order*, where no one has privacy, and critical thinking is reduced to zero. Everything would be regulated by supercomputers telling you what to do and what to think. In the end, they make you believe that intelligence is above all else— to the point where we forget how to love, even to love ourselves with our imperfections… Now, it turns out that we can't even be *absolutely perfect*—as if perfection itself were a sin or an offense to those controlling the narrative.

A procession of radicalized, normalized, and indoctrinated individuals who have lost their soul and motivation, having been completely *absorbed*. Frankly, the whole thing is a bit terrifying. Fear paralyzes—but don't let yourself be paralyzed in such interesting and complex times. You are here to *be*, not to speculate!!

Plutocracy is a rather unpalatable reality. The year 2024 is an 8 *year*, and Pluto remains in the third decan of Capricorn—a long transit through Gate 60, where we will witness limitations, mutations, and *death!!*

My reflection in this chapter is the following: what will happen the day the network is no longer operational? The internet could very well cease to be "reality." In fact, *Ra* already predicted this, and at this point, I trust *him* more than any influencer, journalist, or postmodern philosopher.

It seems that no one is considering that we are approaching 2027, and we are all part of this multidimensional *Odyssey* where DNA plays a crucial role. We must remember that updating your code takes an estimated *seven years*, but it can be accelerated if one consciously decides and commits to oneself. But don't rush—it's not a race of toads. *Piano, piano si va lontano*, right? *Patience.*

Many of us know and desire a decentralized and alternative economy— one that is sustainable and coherent. If we don't at least envision a *minimally interesting* new scenario, an escalation of war is inevitable (*war always returns*).

Things are not looking good, but we must remain optimistic and believe that there are people capable of protecting the ecosystem, childhood, values, and *the good life.* Few truly commit to *being*—self-sabotage, lack of self-love, and absence of personal responsibility and commitment are evident…

Personally, I would invest in those supporting cannabis: *PotCoin, CannabisCoin, ParagonCoin, HempCoin,* and *CannaCoin!!*

Some demand freedom, yet they are incapable of imagining themselves free from mental patterns and absurd thoughts… nor do they truly want others to be free, because that would seem like *"le fin du monde."*

And here we are… mediocrity has taken hold of the planet, along with indifference, the *"plan"demic,* and war!! A complete mess. How is it that Coca-Cola is legal while marijuana is not!!??

Cannabis is likely one of the key factors in combating climate change— without a doubt, a solid investment. Right now, it's a 3 *trillion USD* market, already linked to the crypto world!

We are witnessing a *colossal revolution*. The effects of cryptocurrency are as transformative as those of the internet or mobile phones. Until now, the economy as we know it has been sustained by physical assets like land, but it seems that resource has been *depleted*.

However, with *Jupiter's entry into an Air sign—Aquarius,* things will take on a whole new dimension. It is estimated that this shift will become effective, real, and tangible by 2023.

Obviously, Bitcoin is part of this new paradigm.

Welcome to the Age of Aquarius—or not!!

Pluto in Capricorn is deeply cryptic (*Cripto,* the god of hidden treasures). The fact that Pluto entered Capricorn (*institutions/ governments*) is an undeniable sign and reality of the destruction of the system as we know it. In fact, Pluto is set to enter Aquarius around the end of 2023!

Meanwhile, Saturn has moved into Pisces… and the *"conspiracy"* is becoming evident. Saturn has the power to crystallize things—slowly but powerfully. It is *Cronos, the god of time…*

Yes, *the whole planet* is thinking about the same topic, consciously or unconsciously. Many of us believe that things must take a turn. And if you pull hard in one direction, I…

The *blockchain* will inevitably impose itself. But perhaps we are walking straight into the wolf's mouth. Blockchain makes the system *"very secure"* because all computers control it collectively. It is an underlying technology, not just a currency—more of a *philosophy* or *modus operandi,* a new way of negotiating and trading.

A smart, self-regulating currency where users are involved and *"control"* the game… It's a *peer-to-peer (P2P)* system, a *2-to-2* exchange with no notaries (*mining*), eliminating banks, states, and intermediaries.

In reality, the system is collapsing on its own. Today, it is part of the problem, and the *solution* seems *"interesting"*!

That's why governments are buying Bitcoin—to control it or soften the blow??

Blockchain leaves no trace, yet it is transparent and holds infinite possibilities… It evolves on its own, and it's already in motion—it's *unstoppable.*

Bitcoin is trading on the stock market *against the US dollar*!

China, *Saturnian,* is the first major global player in blockchain… In truth, it's all very experimental, just like the internet was in its early days.

Will it *stick?*

What happens if there's an unexpected failure in the network?

No one sees it coming, obviously… but maybe it's inevitable.

I'm just saying—*consider this a warning!!*

Uranus entered Taurus in April 2019…

All of this is taking on a significant dimension—the way we understand money is changing radically, as is its intrinsic value. It will move into Gemini in 2025, and things will change *drastically…* We're shifting from the *earth element* to the *air element*!!

The value of the euro-dollar is unstable because it is not backed by anything—not even gold!

Who absorbed the shock of the crisis?? We all did. The state didn't, because at this point, it is outdated and severely weakened—just like all of us!! In fact, it is completely lost; it must reinvent itself or disappear... It is resisting the *mutation-extinction* that we are destined to experience, which is, in fact, *inevitable.*

Right now, it has little credibility—it merely reproduces an *anachronistic pattern.* However, since inertia is powerful, it will continue to exist... or at least *pretend* to!!

Throughout 2020, we witnessed the *Saturn-Jupiter conjunction in Aquarius,* which will set long-term trends. And with the *Uranus square,* the *New Order* comes to an end—along with the fall of an *elite*!

The old elite (*ruled by Taurus, an earth sign*) is resisting the new paradigm and the decentralization of the system.

The system, in general, is in crisis—it is neither self-sufficient nor credible. It is rotting from within, and *Pluto is bearing witness to this.*

Blockchain is a shared database—it is the new way to distribute and conduct transactions. The *currency* will have more flexibility, and more people will be involved.

By then, we will be working with *quantum computers,* and the digitization of money will be a fully accomplished fact.

Bitcoin is a currency with more than two sides and various purposes, depending on how it is interpreted. As of now, it remains an *enigma*—it is a medium of exchange that no one prints, but rather is created through a network of interconnected computers!!

It meets three basic requirements to be considered a currency:

- It is a **medium of exchange**
- It is a **unit of value**
- It is a **store of value**, allowing for savings

Its value has skyrocketed—since January 2017, Bitcoin has increased by **1000%**, even reaching peaks that have **revalued it by 2000% in less than a year...**

Mining

Mining Bitcoin means generating currency through mathematical operations that search for a **random 256-bit number**, which must be *equal to or lower* than the number assigned to the given block.

Once the number is found, the miner earns a block, which at that moment is worth **12.5 bitcoins.**

Every **four years**, the block size is **halved** to increase mining difficulty—this, in turn, drives up Bitcoin's value.

The Bitcoin mining **script** is programmed so that the **maximum limit of 21 million bitcoins** will not be reached until **2040.**

Every **15 days**, the system checks how long it took to mine the blocks and adjusts the difficulty of the mathematical problem accordingly—ensuring that the mining rate remains **one block every 10 minutes.**

The computers or nodes responsible for mining also earn Bitcoins by performing the function of **verifying Bitcoin transactions** between users. These transactions are recorded in the **ledger**, which is the blockchain, and in return, the miners receive a portion of the transaction fee.

Scalability

Since each Bitcoin block is **limited to 1 megabyte**, the number of verified transactions per second **cannot exceed seven**. This limitation affects Bitcoin's usability, as sometimes transaction confirmations take **hours or even days**, losing the **instant transfer capability** it initially had.

To address this issue, various solutions have been proposed:

- **SegWit** (Segregated Witness) attempted to increase block size to **2 megabytes**, but even that would be insufficient.
- Currently, tests are being conducted with the **Lightning Network**, which aims to handle **many more transactions per second at lower costs**. This would restore Bitcoin's appeal as a **medium of exchange**, since transaction verification delays and increasing costs had turned it more into a **store of value** rather than an exchange currency.

Blockstream & Control Over Bitcoin

Blockstream is the platform that controls Bitcoin's **original code**, and it is suspected of **manipulating or interfering with Bitcoin's scalability** to make its usage **less attractive**.

Blockstream received a **$55 million investment** from **AXA Group**, which was led by one of the **top figures in the Bilderberg Club**.

This suggests that **Bitcoin was not outright banned**, but rather, it is being **controlled**.

Years ago, **Circle**, a payment transfer company controlled by **Goldman Sachs**, purchased **Poloniex** (one of the leading cryptocurrency exchanges) for **$400 million**.

The fact that **major financial groups are making high-value investments** to enter the crypto sector strongly suggests that **Bitcoin will not be banned, but it will be regulated.** These financial giants are **positioning themselves** to capitalize on this **emerging market.**

At the last **G20 meeting,** a ban on Bitcoin was ruled out, but **upcoming regulations were discussed.** Countries like **Japan** already recognize Bitcoin as a **legal currency,** and **Germany** has recently implemented regulations, which could serve as a **guideline** for other European Union member states.

Decentralization or Not?

In the end, it will be **the citizens themselves,** through their support, who decide whether to continue trusting **centralized systems** or reclaim their **financial sovereignty.**

It is likely that those currently **in power** will attempt to **create chaos in the markets,** only to later introduce a **state- or central bank-controlled cryptocurrency** as the solution. This is a **common strategy**—first create a problem, then sell the solution.

A Consciousness Shift Toward a Decentralized Society?

Could this be a step toward a **decentralized society?** Perhaps. But at the same time, **we might be obsessively magnifying reality!!!**

Also, I want to **issue a warning**—at some point, **before or after 2027, the Internet could collapse and cease to exist!!**

Nikolái Roerich

(29)

Free energy-free your self

Scalar Electric Waves were named and discovered by the brilliant and beloved engineer Nikola Tesla. With the coils from patent 512,340, Tesla managed to neutralize self-induction and isolate the magnetic field from electrical energy. He discovered the existence of scalar waves and/ or radiant energy.

By filtering out Hertzian waves, only radiant waves remain—a type of energy that nature uses to generate space-time. Everything vibrates, everything has a wave; the vibration emitted by any person, object, or unit, such as a flower or a plant, is radiant energy—scalar electric waves propagating through space-time as frequencies.

This vibration is the sum of its parts, as force or energy originates within each particle or quantum of reality.

We open three R&D (Research & Development) documents on Tesla and Patent 685,957: Method of Utilizing Radiant Energy (https://goo. gl/ya6dQx) and Patent 512,340 (https://goo.gl/Pta1Rs).

Here, the Bifilar Coil holds the key to harmonic resonance. It functions like an electro-plasmatic flux capacitor, capable of cooling electrical energy from the power grid to separate magnetism and electricity. The result? The cosine of Phi of the energy consumed approaches zero, meaning 100% energy savings and the ability to generate a fresh, safe, natural, and non-hazardous form of electrical energy.

How? What? Yes!! It is cold electrical energy that comes from the ether, according to Nikola Tesla... The Ether is cosmic electricity, a pre-matter state from which plasma emerges: it consists of three electronic force lines (two with opposite polarity and one neutral) that combine into six facets (a cube) with twelve polarities and a center.

From this variety, seven fundamental types of plasma are formed—the building blocks of reality.

The seven chakras interact with the seven plasmas, which contain the frequency and vibration—energy and information—necessary for life, a creative power that generates nine dimensions of time, which we recognize as the Mind.

This knowledge can be accessed through the Galactic History or Galactic Yoga (https://13lunas.net/SYNCHRONOTRON.htm), a system through which the paranormal abilities of humanity become the norm.

The conclusion is that gravity is a scalar wave, vectorial and tensional, containing information and energy (power). Like the other two waves—magnetic and electric—it is also triple: 3x3=9; this is Nikola Tesla's 3, 6, 9 code.

A triple universe, which he described as:

- Phenomenal,
- Imaginal,
- Moral,

where inverse symmetry generates six planes of a Space-Time cube with nine interior dimensions (6+6 represents polarity).

The Gravitational plane maintains a triple polarity (above and below) within the Space-Time cube, along with the other two electromagnetic planes:

- Electromagnetic (double polarity)
- Biopsychic (neutral, without polarity, at the center of rotation or charge spin—the center of the cyclone or hurricane).

We already knew that three are the electrical force lines of the Aether, which polarize into the Flower of Life (6+6=12 combinations) to form 7 Radial Plasmas essential for life.

Three electronic force lines of ether:

- Two with opposite polarity (Kuali-red & Duar-blue)
- One neutral.

See: Cosmic Science (https://goo.gl/JfG4F2) & I+D Blog (https://goo.gl/76wyQ5).

The Radial Plasmas can be identified with the magma at Earth's center, as they are conducted from an origin point near the center of the galaxy, passing through Earth's poles to its crystalline core (Crystal Earth 12, Kin 137, Ah Vuc Ti Cab's realm in the Mayan worldview).

Plasma is a fluid composed of electrically charged particles, within which lie the basic building blocks of reality. Radial plasma is the origin of the state of matter; in scientific terms, plasma is a state of matter where almost all atoms are ionized, with the presence of a certain number of free electrons, not bound to any atom or molecule.

In 2016, the existence of these waves was officially confirmed by science—they are called Gravitational Waves, and scientists claim that Einstein was right: there exists an energy released by certain supermassive celestial objects, such as the Galactic Center (Hunab Ku). This, in our understanding, forms the "triple binary polarity" of the particle known as the Graviton.

Therefore, everything designed by Nikola Tesla works, as his inventions are based on scalar energy, including gravitational waves, magnetic waves, and electric waves. These are, ultimately, part of the triple wave of the Fifth Force, also known as the Galactic Force or Force G, as proposed by the Planetary Art Network and envisioned by the "Jedis" of the Galactic Federation.

Light energy, photon cyclone, emerges from the center, as the force that connects everything—the fifth force that unifies the four fundamental forces (Gravity, Electromagnetic, Strong Nuclear, and Weak Nuclear). It is an intelligent force that we call Radial Plasma.

The great Third Hermetic Principle (the Principle of Vibration) states that motion is present throughout the universe: nothing is at rest, everything vibrates and spins (Nothingness is concentrated creative mind).

This scalar or radiant wave energy was later called Orgone Energy by Wilhelm Reich. Throughout history, this vibrational energy has been given many names:

- Chi (China)
- Ki (Japan)
- Mungo (Africa)
- Ka (Egypt)

- Mana (New Zealand, Hawaii, Papua New Guinea, Easter Island)
- Prana / Kundalini (India)
- Tumo (Tibet)
- Baraka (Sufis)
- Dynamis, Pneuma (Ancient Greece)
- Vital Force or Fifth Essence (Alchemists)
- Astral Light (Kabbalists)
- Pleroma (Gnostics)
- Ether (Aristotle)

This virtue or energy can be developed through Plasma technology.

Research & Development: https://goo.gl/48YpKo

Gravity, electromagnetism, and spirituality are qualities of Plasma, detected as energy waves and vibrational information that take the form of scalar, vectorial, and tensional geometries.

Scalar electric waves—Tesla's great discovery! He used them to obtain free energy or zero-point energy.

Cells in organic systems communicate with each other through scalar magnetic waves (Meylian waves), both inside and outside the body.

Everyone acknowledges that fractality is an infinite understanding—see the Mandelbrot formulas or the holographic mathematics of the Mayan Code (as explained in *The Mayan Factor* book).

Fractal mathematics teaches us the mathematics of infinite understanding, but no one knew that a FRACTAL FIELD existed (scalar, vectorial, and tensional).

The Golden Ratio, the Divine Proportion, is undoubtedly optimized self-similarity, just as fractality itself is.

Our heart has an electromagnetic pulse that amplifies its triple conjugated wave with the Schumann phase, which is in resonance with the Galactic Center. This not only creates the dynamic torsion (spin) of the DNA spiral but also influences the mental and atmospheric climate of Gaia, emerging from the same fractal field—or chaos—since, to some extent, the fractal field represents supreme order, where love has a place, is perceived, and is enjoyed depending on one's alignment!

Einstein argued that gravity was an infinite comprehension of charge, but he never learned that it was a fractal. Now, try to imagine that energy is Time, meaning that our Mind is Factorizing Art into the phenomenal electromagnetic Space, which is synchronized with the other two realms: the imaginal (biopsychic) and the moral (mental). Meylians or the magnetic field of Fascenic Lines.

P.S.: Gravity is a mental plane, so levitation is possible. The Law of Levitation states: Less materialistic egoism = More lightness, Less mental density = More mental emptiness = Less noise = More natural consciousness/mind = Entry into resonance with Earth's scalar, vectorial, and tensional wave = Possibility of moving with the whole body. Follow the count of the days and the 13 moons of 28 days = Tesla's patent spiral = Universal Harmonic Constant (7x4 = 28).

Gravity, electromagnetism, and spirituality are qualities of Plasma detected as vibrational energy and information waves, which are mathematical or scalar, vectorial, and tensional geometries, respectively. Scalar electric waves were Tesla's great discovery!

Cyber document link: https://goo.gl/c5VsNp

Conclusion:

Gravitational energy is therefore radiant; it originates from the center and radiates in all directions. The mental plane is gravitational, within the previously described triple-universe model.

Electricity can be demagnetized, and polarity can be tuned to the radial frequency of gravity or the galactic G-force. Gravitational energy is the energy an object possesses due to its position within a gravitational field. The most common use of gravitational potential energy occurs in objects near the Earth's surface, where gravitational acceleration can be assumed to be constant at 9.8 m/s^2.

Since the zero point of gravitational potential energy can be defined at any chosen location (similar to selecting the zero of a coordinate system), the potential energy at a given height is equal to the work required to lift an object to that height without a net change in its kinetic energy. Given that the force needed to lift an object is equal to its weight, gravitational potential energy is equal to its weight multiplied by the height it is lifted!

The general expression for gravitational potential energy arises from the law of gravity and is equal to the work done against gravity to bring a mass to a specific point in space. Due to the inverse-square nature of the gravitational force, the force approaches zero at large distances, making it logical to choose the zero point of gravitational potential energy at an infinitely distant location. As a result, gravitational potential energy near a planet is negative, since gravity performs positive work when a mass moves closer.

This negative potential indicates a "bound state"—once a mass is near a large body, it is trapped until something supplies enough energy for it to escape.

The three-dimensional mind perceives that "time slips away, slips away, slips away" into the future. But this flowing time is merely a linear perception of time. In the near future, we will experience the convergence of many timelines: dimensional shift. From a higher four-dimensional perspective, time and space are an inseparable unit, and together they form a cube. The three dimensions of space-time (length, width, and height) are united by the invisible cube of time, which is the fourth dimension:

- Time = Fourth Dimension
- Mind = Gravitational Plane

As long as life and its auxiliary cosmological processes function in accordance with the normative values of time and its synchronizing frequency 13:20, the space-time cube remains relatively constant.

For the perceptions of multidimensional beings immersed in the vast space-time cube of cosmic reality, the dimensions of this cube have no limits. This is because no matter where you go, you are always at the center of this giant cube. Such is the nature of the cosmocentric perspective intrinsic to cosmic consciousness!

However, when there is a deviation from the harmony of living in accordance with the universal values of the synchronization frequency, distorted perceptions begin to affect the space-time cube.

When these distorted perceptions arise from the limiting effects of living solely by three-dimensional beliefs conceptualized in the 12:60 time frequency, then life exceeds all limits and expands convulsively at phenomenological speed rates toward the extremes of its own space-time cube!

Heart Coherence

In summary, the scientific reason for living in heart coherence is that, among all the scientific theories that emerged in the 20th century, the most relevant and useful to humanity is the one stating that the entire universe is interconnected and coherent.

Coherence implies order, structure, harmony, and alignment within and between systems—whether atoms, living organisms, social groups, planets, or galaxies. Most people know what it feels like to be in a state of harmonic alignment... in this state, our heart, mind, and body are integrated and united. Everything becomes possible because everything is dynamic, and everything has its own unique rhythm!

I want to express my gratitude to Iván Ugido Martínez for his work and for trusting me with his research. However, I must mention that he is currently seeking financial support to launch a pilot project.

José Argüelles – ValumVotan

30

Personal Reflection on How I Interpret a Calendar Within Parameters That May Seem Paranormal

Time must be lived and enjoyed… Without balance, nothing becomes a sacred work or a mystery in itself. *Time is Art* (Argüelles, *The Law of Time*).

The first thing I believe is important to point out is that the astral year always begins on January 21st, when the Sun transits through Gate 60 and jumps to Gate 41. Here, everything "magically" ends, and everything begins anew with a diminution and an emanation of life, bringing with it an unexpected burden or obligation—to be born again… Life is like that, an experiment and a journey!

But let's be *lunatics* and allow ourselves to be guided by the one celestial body that moves and stirs us from within, provoking all kinds of emotions—the Moon!

Everything spins, everything moves. This cannot be ignored. Sometimes time speeds up, and sometimes it seems like absolutely nothing is happening, yet everything is constantly changing, especially during planetary retrogrades, which trigger *déjà vu* moments or unsettling situations.

It is crucial to understand the role you play in this dynamic and dual system, perfectly orchestrated in a mathematical way. Perhaps God is the one accompanying us on this strange, dangerous, mysterious, and starry journey…

Some have seen divinity in plants, constellations, abstract or conceptual art… Others have gone even further, or have simply been able to recognize a pattern that keeps us connected in a fractal and holistic way… In chaos, there is order, and also beauty!

Let's Talk About Numbers!

Everything has a numerical pattern—absolutely everything. Words, geometry, music, and the human body all follow a numerical order. The key is to approach it intelligently, without prejudice or resistance. It would be wise to relax, make an effort, and step out of the Matrix for a moment to truly see and experience the mystery firsthand. Open your eyes and play… A good attitude and a willingness to challenge yourself against reality are essential. Accepting that not knowing is a very healthy state—the exact opposite of believing you know everything and thinking like everyone else.

There are so many reactive individuals obsessed with being "free" that it's almost sad to see such normalized and programmed ignorance, endlessly repeating the same suspicious evolutionary pattern. It's uninspiring! Isn't it time to transcend this repressed and dormant reality? Don't waste your time on bourgeois frogs looking down on you. They have no soul—just clocks and an urgent need for control. Keep your distance and take action because everything is constantly shifting and transforming!

Time is relative, but let's not waste it. We have no time to lose on outdated norms, obsolete theories, or endless principles. Instead, let's enjoy and participate in synchronicities, which give everything color and music!

Shall we play at being gods? Let everyone play the game they find most meaningful, but never forget that without spirit, one suffocates alone for lack of soul—and ultimately fails.

Life is that powerful and wild. And if you don't understand something, life will teach you—because at a spiritual level, you are a soul living in the material plane. Let's not forget: our body is a temple, not just a bicycle. It has its own biological rhythm and demands our full attention—so tune in!

Personally, I suggest living in non-linear time—a circular-spiral-spiritual experience where the harmonic frequency is 13:20, not 12:60.

Art is such a sublime exercise that, once you've harmonized your life, it will allow you to perceive and live in a "plusquam-perfect" dimension. It's about enjoying time. *Tao* is the law of no-time and simplicity—and if we can flow in the immediate present, everything will naturally unfold. It seems complex because we have lost our connection with the natural world and with ourselves.

Perhaps it's your rational perception, conditioned by an outdated culture, that weighs you down like a heavy burden. Let go. Jump into infinity. Trust yourself and trust life. Anything can happen—in fact, everything will happen! And at some point, you may start questioning what role you're meant to play.

You must take responsibility and decide if you are truly the one navigating this vast blue ocean—where the stars continue to flicker!

In fact, it is impossible to renounce paradise—it's not so far away. Maybe you've already been there but have stopped dreaming… Remember God and lift your head; it's wonderful if you open your eyes. You only live once, so wake up and observe carefully—the spectacle is infinite.

Yes, it's a cosmic joke—whether you understand it or not. We walk and open unknown or sealed dimensions. With humor and good vibes, anything can happen. Don't rush—it's not a race, it's a multi-dimensional experience. We are self-reflecting consciousness, mirrors and filters of awareness. As the Latins said: *Amor Omnia Vincit*—love conquers all.

The Greeks built a temple in Delphi where an oracle proclaims: *Nosce te ipsum*—know yourself. A maxim that can keep you inspired for a lifetime—what more could you ask for? I mean, this is where it all begins—if you're ready for your journey.

At that exact geographic location, two green eagles, released by Apollo from opposite ends of the world, crossed paths—at Delphi.

Time is a master you cannot escape. You must learn to locate yourself in the vastness, just as the wise men of the East, mystics, alchemists, emperors, and astrologers have always done. But they didn't have the navigational coordinates that you have now—ones that allow you to understand, assimilate, and truly enjoy. So get ready!

The *carte du ciel*, as the French say, is essential. Just think—one day, in a precise and precious instant, your mother gave birth to light (you must experience darkness to see the stars). And this light is still alive as long as you breathe. If that's the case, go back to the beginning and realize that you are truly one of the fortunate ones among millions, in an absolutely beautiful and magical world.

The entire universe conspires for you to be who you are—and that alone is a privilege. Prepare yourself for the changing seasons, rainy days, stormy seas, and bohemian nights. To touch the sky with your hands and see what no one has seen before. For long, slow afternoons with the wind at your back. If you step outside, a starry sky awaits you, while the rooster crows and the turtles carry on… everything has its time.

Everything requires a certain level of complicity—slow and steady wins the race. And if you are capable of understanding yourself and living your destiny, you will also understand that everything has a rhythm and an explicit meaning—everything.

But if you choose not to live it, you'll just experience a soulless reproduction of life—or worse, you'll find yourself lost in the Matrix.

Do you want to be a fish outside the fishbowl?

According to the I-Ching, as soon as we let go of our identity, possibilities become infinite. This does not mean that life is easy—on the contrary. But it becomes much more mysterious and interesting if you trust the Tao.

Complexity requires simplicity, and only with intuition, time, and conviction in our own nature can we open ourselves to the vastness of this strange, sometimes incomprehensible game. Yes, everything is a dream, an illusion, or a chimera. Perhaps we will have to "surrender" to form and to the evidence…

We are vulnerable and fragile—time passes… step by step, slowly, gently, lovingly, we can reinvent ourselves. Because this is coming to an end, and it's not the end of the world!

Cosmic history is not an operetta; it is the beginning of something we will experience firsthand. But what is certain is that beginnings are always difficult. Chaos is inevitable, but we do not have a choice. However, if one understands the game, perhaps one day they will become its protagonist—or even a poem.

Maybe being reborn will be painful, but there is no turning back. You may end up alone—or not—but everything is as it should be. You will have to accept the challenge of understanding that hardship and trials are unequivocal signs of transformation—both of the self and of the universe. We are the ones who program the Maya.

Shall we talk about deterministic chaos? Shall we enter Daaz? "If you don't want dust, don't go to the threshing floor. And if you don't cry, you don't get fed!" Now I look back, because the Renaissance was the result of an absolute and perfectly contextualized worldview in its time. Some imagined the splendor of Florence, Pisa, or Tuscany. Humanists have always been persecuted, controversial, polemical, and authentic—because they stir the past and seek progress. Today, we have Eden within reach—maybe we are already there, but we are not aware of it! Still, we are living through a historically intense moment—sometimes sublime—but the great enemy is as real as it is ruthless: indifference, the dictatorship of mediocrity, and the cowardly attitudes of those who neither moan nor sigh. Let's be a little intelligent. Staying in the Matrix is collective suicide in slow motion. And the system as we know it will end in 2027. Cosmic history is already in motion. Its moment of initiation was July 26, 2013. So let's enjoy the months of 28 moons!

The Sinchronary/Tzolkin allows us to break free from a "reality" that has become nearly psychotic or bipolar—where the result is the normalization of the norm itself. We can understand that time is art through practice and a certain elegance; it's about embracing a parallel, distinct, and unique reality—one that might seem wrong to others. We nourish and rediscover ourselves because we are all connected, mathemagically or spiritually. It would be wise to understand that we are one single entity (the Earth), living one single time, as one single people—yet we are different, and this difference enriches us. With time, you can understand or comprehend. Knowledge will set us free—or maybe not—but dare to dream! Everything depends on many factors, but don't try to control them, because life is a mysterious and wonderful game, and time is a decisive factor. Don't let anyone steal your time or impose agendas on you. Now, a red star has fallen into the sea. It's an owl-filled night, and the snails are coming out! From now on, you will never again be so harsh or so "normal"—nor so gullible, nor so intelligent, nor so vain. Perhaps, one day, the moon will appear yellow against a black sky—just as you have already imagined or consciously projected. Remember that we program the Maya. We are living beings, animated by binary consciousness, and we move! Never forget: the mystery is unfathomable, and you are a part of it—if you recognize that you are dreaming inside a dream, and that the dream is dreaming you! Learn to be yourself and to love your dreams—you never know. They say the muses appear while you work… And you—are you already dancing? Don't lose the rhythm!

31

Figs from another basket

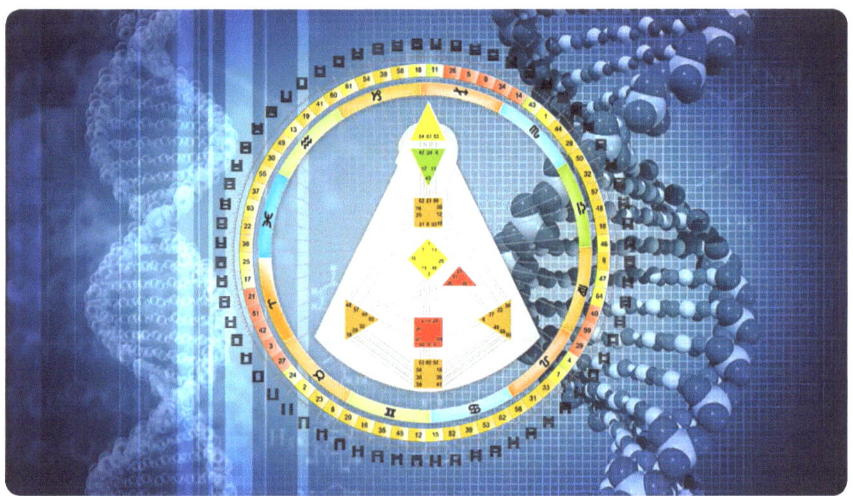

Do you really know how to eat? Do you really know who you are first thing in the morning?

Before "sitting at the table" and attacking, you need to be in sync and present… Think about it—eating is, by nature, a wild act, even a violent one, but it has its own mystique and a science that allows for good digestion!

Yes, eating an apple is a whole challenge; it requires stopping, meditating, breathing, and enjoying… But there are many ways to approach a plate of rice with rabbit—and to cook it—but that's another topic!

The problem is that today's gastronomic culture is a very "interesting" religion. Religion denies us a unique and distinct way of being, so we all end up eating the consecrated host, turning paradise into a valley of tears… or not!

We are love, and we shouldn't be guinea pigs… Love however you want, but don't forget to look at yourself in the mirror every day. Maybe *you* are the love of your life—if you learn to be yourself and nourish yourself in your own unique way!

It's not about devouring the world—quite the opposite. Otherwise, we'll end up overfed and overwhelmed by a slice of cake of dubious origin… Learning to eat is a real challenge; it's part of personal growth, an experiment, or a celebration, depending on how you look at it… pure alchemy or a bad trip.

It must be said that eating is not a cultural act—not at all. In fact, it's a journey that deserves your presence and commitment because it shapes your cognition. If you commit to it, don't doubt that your body will tone up and sing to the four winds. If you do it right, your mind will change— you'll be much more "eloquent" and/or versatile. As the poet said, there are still songs to be sung beyond humankind!

Much has been said about nutrition—too much, in fact. Personally, I think it has reached an absurd level because everyone has an opinion, and everyone speaks their mind. But the homogenization of culinary culture only leads to long faces, obesity, and malnutrition: some people go hungry while others don't even know how to eat!

In general, we're facing a serious problem because we're overindulging and normalizing a reality without limits. The "stir-fry" is starting to stink, or it's becoming indigestible because people simply don't know how to eat!

Consider the option of living and enjoying a personalized/optimal digestion—it requires knowing just four things!

First of all, let me say that I have a refined palate. I've tried all kinds of cuisine, including the best, and I've also witnessed substantial improvements in the way I live, see, and think thanks to the Primary Health System (PHS)!

The Primary Health System allows you to experience a reality that is not standardized—almost sublime. A good digestion will alter your perspective and motivation. Likewise, the environment and conditions influence the entire process immensely!

Can you imagine a half-mad architect in the kitchen, eagerly cooking to please his child at the table?

At home, my mother and father cooked without limits. Sometimes, five or six dishes would come out, prepared with love, care, and patience! A true joy—I can't even begin to explain the details. It's a tradition that shapes a life or even an entire family—a serious matter! But I must also say that, physically, I wasn't in great shape, and intellectually, I was quite limited—maybe due to poor digestion!

My madness has always been evident around a cooking pot. At the table, I have the soul of an alchemist. But what surprises me most now is my ability to keep hacking life in truly unbelievable ways. I put a huge dose of imagination into life. I feel increasingly clear-headed and satisfied, and I eat better and better in every sense—mainly because I have found the perfect cooking point to have the morning vigor I need!

Now I know how to eat, and my body and mind are grateful for it!

I was never picky, nor was I a catalog gourmet—no, I ate because it was part of the ritual, and the ritual made me happy (I would cry from joy). But I have now moved beyond that phase; living well and better concerns me more and more. I have learned elementary things that keep my physical and mental health in check—they call it prevention and/or awareness.

Now I eat half as much, in optimal conditions, and my performance has improved remarkably.

I mean that I am increasingly aware of what truly benefits me—and also of what I don't need. I have become more discerning; I now know how to keep my body (hardware) happy, and my software does its job seamlessly. It's a binomial relationship that must always be kept in mind: we are merely passengers, the body is the vehicle, and it is what truly experiences life!

Everything has its process and requires maximum attention. Sleeping alone and eating according to your hologenetic profile are crucial—a luxury available to everyone. Silence, too, is considered a luxury nowadays. It is essential for processing consciousness itself. In stillness, one can understand things; let's not forget that we are self-reflecting consciousness!

If you know yourself, you love yourself, and the effects are remarkable. If you are radical in your transformation, you will realize that taking care of your health means living consciously and eating according to your PHS (Primary Health System)! It is, in fact, very simple, but without commitment and common sense, no real improvements will take place.

If the process is carried out correctly, you will begin to live in fullness and balance—and your presence will become truly noticeable!

To give you an example, personally, I have to consider three things when I prepare to process a meal (or information):

1. I need direct sunlight while I eat.
2. I need altitude.
3. I need to savor every bite through my nose—I have to smell and inhale what I eat, and this excites my little brain enormously!

From there, I can eat anything because my digestive system is modern! In this sense, I can digest all kinds of food, but not everyone has this type of digestive system. We all have very different ways of approaching this experience. However, not everyone is truly prepared to understand that eating without criteria normalizes and conditions people massively (leading to homogeneous thinking as both cause and effect).

In the process of differentiation, one must face certain aspects radically and without prejudice. Following trends or diets won't get us far! We all know that, at the table, we should try everything—or not—but people don't evolve in their process and continue making digestion impossible!

Diversity is necessary and very rewarding, but we are all becoming more alike due to a lack of personal criteria and coherence in our eating habits. The result? More normalization, more standardization—we look like zombies in line, wasting fortunes and precious time for nothing.

If we aren't conscious of this, we don't enter correctly into the experience, and digestion is terrible. If we don't contextualize it properly, we end up with a bad experience (and it's not the chef's or the restaurant's fault). However, we must fix this so that the revolution/transformation can be definitive and optimal.

It's true that innovation is a great indicator in all aspects of life, but without consciousness, the results are disastrous. People spend fortunes on courses, diets, and high-quality products, yet mealtime conversations are getting duller and more meaningless by the day. The planet is heating up due to bad practices, and algorithms are starting to dictate a life without solid, balanced, and sensitive values.

Yes, we have lost our way. Everything is too mental, everything is accelerating—and now 5G has arrived!

I remember one Christmas, I saw a horrifying photo of a holiday dinner table, where €500 bills sat next to €200 bills, alongside party hats and dirty ashtrays. The scene was pathetically "cheap", and I thought, *This is the perfect image of the nouveau riche fool*—the kind of person who spends €4,000 or even €8,000 to feed just eight people!

Then you stop and think—you realize that out on the streets, there are people freezing, with nothing but a frozen carrot for lunch.

We all know that after-dinner conversations can sometimes be suspicious, dull, or strange—and sometimes downright unbearable. Everyone talks about the same old things to avoid the truth… football, politics, or some postcard-perfect vacation spot where they can park their asses—and their souls.

It doesn't matter how fancy or prestigious you are—what really matters is the desire to live, to laugh, and to share the journey with those you love… beyond clichés and the fears of some soul-less, scared little bourgeois. But let's not forget the "coca-cola-drinking normies" who bore us with their bad taste and lack of sensitivity at the table—or anywhere else, for that matter.

The dullness and sadness disguised as happiness have become an epidemic that is polluting and overheating the planet. It's shameful—this generalized ignorance and indifference. Yes, the dictatorship of mediocrity and vanity is now the standard currency of society. It's the misery of a "happy" world, hyper-connected yet submissive to trends and artificial substitutes.

In general, this is a colossal failure—leading to the destruction of both the planet and human beings themselves. People have lost their spirit because they no longer know how to think—or even how to eat! They simply devour everything, then shit it out however they can.

Artificial substitutes and appearances have become the ultimate values—because people don't know how to truly live, nor how to truly eat. It seems like they're eating money itself—and sometimes even the packaging too!

Money as the supreme reality is a frankly disgusting trend. It's honestly embarrassing—and a little terrifying.

We are heading in the wrong direction. The beer is getting warm, the women are getting cold, the children are crying, and the mothers are desperately searching for help on their phones—because the system protects no one. It's obsolete, and it only has a few days left.

As Chomsky says, facts no longer hold any value—and, as Oscar Wilde put it, if you dare to dream, society will never forgive you.

Maybe it would be a good idea to stop for a moment and think about how we "eat"!

Even though eating well is desirable, the real issue is not what we eat, but how we approach it to ensure excellent digestion. That is what makes the difference, what allows us to assimilate nutrients in a unique way, and at the same time, what helps with prevention.

Aren't we all different and unique? Then each of us must understand what conditions and circumstances are most favorable to our own body. It's as simple as that! We need to tune in and identify the coordinates that match our digestive system.

Everyone knows that health is essential—in Catalonia, we have a saying: "Health and money!" But it's actually quite concerning because we delegate even in matters as important as health. We no longer take precautions or practice true prevention. Well, some do!

Being cautious is worth double—or even triple. But we need to approach the issue with determination and commitment. Otherwise, we will never get to the bottom of it and will just keep following routines, diets, and advice dictated by so-called "experts" who look like they have a sour face—or a fridge's backside.

Yet we still listen to them and even pay them a fortune, when most likely, their advice isn't all that useful. We let ourselves be fooled by some "doctor honoris causa" who probably follows outdated medical practices or dietary trends that could actually be inadvisable or even harmful…

Maybe it's time for each person to understand and verify what truly works for their own body and personal health. The fact is, we have been trained to eat based on cultural criteria, following formulas that are probably not even coherent with our own bodies. But because they are endorsed by someone with "authority" in the field, we just give in, delegate responsibility, and adopt formulas or principles that may not be solid or consistent.

We don't know how to eat.

Sure, we all know that "Mediterranean cuisine is one of the best in the world" and that local products are recommended to reduce the environmental impact of food transportation while supporting local producers.

That's great.

And yes, Ayurvedic cuisine, Peruvian food, Chinese gastronomy, and French haute cuisine are all amazing, right?

We lick our fingers and feel like we're in heaven for a while.

But in the long run, it's catastrophic!

The lack of prevention means we end up paying enormous bills (hospitals, doctors) due to a lack of personal responsibility and commitment. Some call it self-sabotage.

At this point, it's clear that we haven't evolved much—or barely at all!

Where are the real after-dinner conversations? Let me explain: I applaud them, but at the same time, I deeply resent them.

I get the feeling that after a fondue or a seafood paella, most diners completely crash, turning as dull as turtles. It's as if grandma's cannelloni had fallen into a black hole.

And I wonder: How is it possible that after eating Palamós prawns, everything remains exactly the same?

Most likely, we're dealing with someone who hasn't properly digested or fully absorbed the experience. Maybe they enjoyed the moment but didn't truly *enter* the experience or process it correctly.

Chances are that after this "trance," the person enters a crisis or contradiction—or falls into fatigue, acid reflux, or mental diarrhea.

The body is incredibly wise, and if you don't provide it with nutrients and vitamins in the right way, it will activate defense mechanisms and remind you that you're a bit of a fool.

Maybe you'll stay in that foolish state for a week or a couple of days, or perhaps you'll end up in bed taking a three-hour nap—and just like that, you've lost an entire day!

These days, the internet is constantly buzzing about something that's an undeniable fact: we have a second brain in our stomach.

The digestive system is highly sophisticated and has clear connections to the brain, right?

Yes, we secrete serotonin—on that, we can all agree.

But we could take it a step further and try to understand that we are not just what we eat—we are also what we see and experience.

We are self-reflective consciousness.

And what really makes the difference is the circumstances and the environment in which we enjoy breakfast or lunch.

For example, I need to eat very little at dinner. But during the day, my brain demands protein, vitamins, and fruit.

In fact, all I truly need is altitude and ultraviolet light—preferably direct exposure—because my digestive system is one of the modern ones.

And when I respect the way my body needs to be nourished, my thinking improves, I enjoy more, and I think less.

It's vital to remember that the mind must follow the body!!??

One of the most essential aspects of life is knowing how to enter well—wherever it may be.

If you enter well, you've already covered a good part of the journey: feeling good, being better, and enjoying the present moment without too many expectations or prejudices.

The same thing applies at the table—exactly the same.

If you know how to enter, you'll leave feeling happy and grateful for life—empowered and improved.

But prejudices are so deeply ingrained that most people will deny themselves the pleasure of taking care of their health.

In the long run, they'll pay the price—big time—either out of irresponsibility or arrogance.

We all have defense mechanisms, but most of them are absurd beliefs that limit our daily lives.

They condition us immensely and restrict us in all areas of life—just because we refuse to face life with awareness and love.

Ra already said it, and I confirm it every day:

You have no choice—you owe yourself to a form.

And if you fail to value yourself, in the end, you'll pay the price—dearly.

Loving and honoring yourself also means recognizing that you are not like everyone else—and not everyone is like you.

Diversity is about understanding your uniqueness while also accepting the differences of others.

Yes, diversity enriches us—but not so much multiculturalism, which in the end has become just another reasonable and acceptable trend that doesn't shine much because we all still follow the same mental and behavioral patterns.

In fact, people eat the same way everywhere.

And if we don't open up to true difference and experience it fully, we end up resenting each other—because nothing truly satisfies us.

The truth is, the problem isn't external—it's internal.

We aren't satisfied with ourselves.

We don't trust life or ourselves.

So we do what is supposedly right—relying on assumptions, excuses, and prejudices that lead nowhere, fueling widespread violence.

And in the end, it's the youngest ones who pay for the meal… and sometimes, the whole "party."

Sociologically speaking, it's becoming increasingly obvious that we are witnessing a rise in indoctrinated democrats, absolute fascism, the dictatorship of mediocrity, cults, and extreme religious movements.It's a serious and undeniable reality. People continue to eat trash and consume without measure.

This global normalization is a highly undesirable "panacea"—it deeply impoverishes us and concerns us all. We are facing a crisis of values that started becoming an epidemic in 2008—and yet, eleven years later, we are still stuck in a deep collective frustration. Sure, it has its moments of joy, drama, and tragedy. But if we look at it closely and critically, this whole epidemic-pandemic could end up being outrageously expensive.

We have smartphones, yet we still struggle to say "good morning. People sleep poorly, eat poorly, and think with their asses!!

We have a blue planet that looks worse every day. We educate our children to become valuable members of society and force them to be better people without actually knowing half of the truth. We don't ask them, and we don't listen to them. There's a palpable sense of dissatisfaction, and eventually, the bomb will explode at home. The kid will demand accountability and either develop violent or unhealthy behaviors or fall into an endless depression due to a lack of reference points or a supportive context. And this is where we are right now: Divided, conflicted, exhausted… conditioned.

The majority of people play the victim role—are we talking about self-sabotage? We get lost in petty details, absurd judgments, and virtual or mental realities that have no real value.People no longer appreciate reality itself or the true value of things—they only know the price of things. For example, the reactive-repressive population gets outraged by the rise of individualism, confusing it with selfishness, and they lose their minds over it!

In some ways, they're not entirely wrong, but they also fail to make a difference. So much fear paralyzes, and love can't breathe. And all of this just because of a non-existent digestion!!

Our collective experience is living its final days—it's running out of time. We are mutating as a species, and nutrition is a key differentiating factor.

What truly matters—what has real, transcendent meaning—is one's personal commitment to oneself and, by extension, to life.

Nowadays, people don't know how to be alone, and they abuse trust. You can be different and create distance in order to live a healthy, coherent, and authentic life. We need to be self-sufficient or interdependent—not constantly at everyone's service all the time!! It's better to understand that we are interdependent—and that dependence is chronic and unhealthy!!

We're not heading in the right direction if we keep eating carelessly. This story is no longer fun—it's a total fake. It was nice, beautiful, and entertaining, but we are at the end of this outdated, soulless "butiflera" reality, lacking respect for diversity. This doesn't mean the world is ending, but we will experience intense moments and social tension.

The coordinates are shifting—both on a macro and micro level. Yes, everything changes, and if you don't make a serious effort to assimilate your immediate present, you'll become a problem for yourself in the long run. And if you don't know how to be alone, when you're older, you'll be unbearable—and difficult to sustain.

Being alone with yourself is quite an experience—if you surrender to your own form. After all, we can't escape ourselves. Sooner or later, we have to face ourselves in the mirror, and if we like what we see, we will dance with the Sun and the Moon. But if we fail to digest life properly or don't learn to navigate it consciously, we'll become nothing more than a fleeting thought, not even a pastime.

We'll be a walking problem, weighed down—literally and figuratively. And no matter how many hours you spend at the gym or how many miracle diets you follow, neither social security nor financial aid will be able to save or reorient you—because the system itself will be out of the game, and so will your immune system.

The same goes for selfishness—some see it as despicable, others as necessary (maybe it's a question of balance?). But the truth is, we've been trained or indoctrinated to be part of the herd, to believe any doctrine or trendy diet—modern, ancient, or millennia-old. Ah, those weight-loss diets!

Thinking for yourself and being selfish is necessary. Now more than ever, we need to be radical—because health is not a game. And neglecting yourself will cost you dearly—in euros and in precious time—and wasting time is a real tragedy. One more thing: society doesn't tolerate free thinkers. Nor does it tolerate artists. Nor skeptics. And much less—dreamers. People dare to attack you if you show vulnerability or difference. (Who even wants to be normal today?)

But if you keep your distance and own your reality with confidence, no one can stop you. In fact, no one can deny you the right to be who you are. (*Now that's true authority.*) We limit ourselves because we don't trust life. And because we don't know how to eat. But—they say no one resists love.

We don't even trust ourselves anymore. We're all starting to look the same, clinging to some repetitive thought that isn't even ours or to some outdated melody without knowing why. We are so conditioned by food that we've become puppets—poor in spirit, living out a sad, forgettable script, just another meaningless number no one will ever remember. (Not that there's any need to remember so much neglect anyway What you leave behind at the end of your journey is up to you. But if you take care of your fragrance, your essence, it will surely resonate in the vastness of existence.

You alone will know your legacy and your final wishes… Who knows? Maybe we're immortal! In any case, one must be bold and live with the commitment to be unique and different—to dance with love, with death, and with those who truly want to live. Those who refuse to enjoy life at the table or in bed? They better stay away.

They can remain plugged into the Neocon Metaverse dictatorship—because when they pull the plug, it's going to be a horror movie. One thing is certain:

Your pleasure at the table, in bed, or at work is the result of your own commitment to yourself—and, in turn, to life itself, to totality.

They say we die the way we live. (That's what they say.) So, enjoy your meal! All of this seems pretty suspicious, doesn't it?

Between fake news, absurd headlines, and general stupidity, we're really on the right track, aren't we?

(Yeah, right. We're headed straight for disaster!)

Sure, we've made progress in many areas—but I'm not so sure.

We're informed about everything, yet we know nothing about ourselves.

(Or very little.)

And we still don't know how to eat intelligently.

Basically, we just repeat and reproduce ourselves in absurd ways.

Some evolve, but very few truly savor existence or embrace the physical, embodied experience of life. Let's not forget: it's the body that lives life. Some live. Some laugh.

And then summer arrives…While others just survive, with a happiness straight out of a catalog.Welcome to the 21st century—where it seems we're either about to give birth to panthers or fry some asparagus.

(Which will it be?)

We are hyper-connected, yet few realize that we are all one. We are all connected, but increasingly isolated, and our vibrational frequency is getting lower and lower, generating fear. People don't know how to be alone and "masturbate" with parallel online realities, pre-cooked meals (or seafood feasts), uncertain futures, or glorious pasts—everything is overly mental, overly rational, and devoid of spirit. Algorithms now tell us how to feel, what to cook, and how to eat, suggesting things so we don't have to think. Maybe we don't even think anymore… or if we do, we think with our ass! Apathy is rampant, and the so-called "normal" people continue their own little sugar-coated party, unwilling to share even a piece of bread. This normalization is insulting and, in part, a result of poor digestion and nutrition. The kleptocracy dominates the planet, unstoppable—what the English call "suckers"—they consume everything, then vomit it back on you and carry on as if nothing happened. Everything is just puritanical fixations and bad digestion. Their cheap way of coexisting is leading us straight to absolute ruin. The dictatorship of mediocrity (not to be confused with poverty—there are mediocre people in every neighborhood) is an undeniable epidemic, and if you don't take a stand, they will devour you like a McDonald's menu item or a plate of frozen green beans. Seeing all this, don't you think you should protect your spirit? But don't forget to be human and love genuinely—one thing doesn't cancel out the other. Prioritize and make decisions accordingly. Changing eating habits isn't easy, but only you can recognize who you are, who you share your table with, and how you consume life itself. There's always something to learn.

You might be skeptical, but simplify—it strengthens you. Make an effort! Be radical in your transformation: first, you need to optimize your hardware to install a next-generation software!

The SPS will help you understand the best conditions for facing a meal, breakfast, or dinner—perhaps dinner isn't advisable (as is my case). We are Homo Sapiens in transit, but we have a very basic mechanics, and understanding this mechanics is essential to assimilating and experiencing a reality that is new every day. Everything changes, everything mutates— but what about you? How do you manage your digestion? Do you know who you are first thing in the morning?

You don't need to change; you just need to accept what you already are and have always been. Reconsider a few fundamental things, find your rhythm, assimilate, love yourself, and recreate yourself! In English, they call it "Shape Shifting" or "Deep Dive"—it's about experiencing in the broadest sense, testing yourself, taking a stand, and coexisting with yourself in the best way possible. Help others if you can, but you must be brave—your life depends on proper digestion!

Eating well, silence, and sleeping alone are, in fact, antidotes against certain realities—a luxury! Everything is fine, but it could be better… You are absolutely "perfect" if you recognize yourself and unlearn habits that don't serve you. It takes time to understand that you are unique and different. You're very close—all you have to do is challenge yourself, walk, listen to your biorhythm, and recognize your geometry, which is not mental. You need to trust in very simple things at first in order to naturally reprogram your DNA. The first 22 days are crucial—once you grasp the basics, you can begin to see, live, and perhaps understand.

One day, you may truly know what your priorities are—your own! However, the SPS cannot be applied indiscriminately. It is a progressive process that requires full attention because it represents a significant change for your body, and it must become aware of what you are suggesting to it. You need to listen carefully, as everything will be perceived differently, and this can create a certain sense of disorientation!

Enjoy as much as you can in your embodied form, respecting your rhythm and your "digestive-nutritional" experience—remember, you have no choice! Self-indulgence is not a good advisor, nor is mental ostracism, indulgence, or indifference. You may know where you are and how you feel, but your mind is probably overwhelmed with countless tasks, topics, or projects. Some people only know how to do things but forget about themselves… they forget to be and to see! In fact, you don't even believe yourself because you keep living in the Non-Self, in the non-being! Be careful not to be deceived!

But if you've made it this far, congratulations! I encourage you to "play," and I wish you good fortune and bon appétit. We cannot deny ourselves good luck, and besides, spring is just around the corner—the almond trees are already blooming, so is the mimosa, and if you make yourself look good, you might even inspire admiration. Who knows? Stranger things have happened!

Maybe you have to dance with the "ugliest" (your mental self), or maybe death is greeting and seeking you—but be brave, because only you can face certain situations, right? Dare to be different, to be yourself at all times, without vanity or self-deception. Don't be a "meatball" who always plays it safe or a frozen croquette—you're unique! If you try to be something you're not, you might disappear in the blink of an eye. But if you stand your ground and take care of yourself with awareness, you will become a great fruit tree. And if you live your own personal mythology, perhaps you will dance without thinking, and your dance will be a precious gift to all who love you. You will share your fruits and your shade when the unbearable heat arrives. Yes, we will come to your place to enjoy everything and nothing, the light and the darkness, and to have a truly memorable digestion!

If life gives you lemons, make lemonade. If you're a fig tree, make fig jam, and we'll eat it while waiting for nightfall—remember, only at night can we see the stars! But if life gives you marijuana… well, you're in luck—it has more benefits than Coca-Cola, and you'll have a good laugh!

In any case, don't try to be someone else. First, focus on being yourself and finding your rhythm. You are not what you eat, nor are you a "crema catalana"—you are unique, you are different, and you have no choice… You are lucky!

Maybe your mental fog is keeping you from truly living or from appreciating what your body is asking for. Maybe listening and unlearning will help you become a better person so that you can feel good about yourself and dance a "cosmic sardana" while whispering sweet words to your neighbor…

Remember, every problem has a solution, but you must address the root causes. That means respecting rhythms without obsessing—some digestions are slow, others are fast, some are difficult, and others are easy. Breathe and trust your instinct, your body—the one that carries you through life. Above all, remember your strategy and your authority!

(32)

The Bio-Solar Non-Egoic Consciousness and the Noospheric Man; Dadaist Poem AUal8

LifeDÀ, the gods, and the spring flowers... children laughing in the streets, dogs gazing absentmindedly at the passage of the green moon, birds soaring ecstatically in the vastness, searching for freedom; rats smoking under a palm tree on a Sunday at noon, church bells ringing because the golden solar sun has risen, and no one knows anything about anything; everything is a wonderful game where one can lose their life if it doesn't rain, and it rains, and the swallows sing because honey drips at dawn, as if colorful manna were falling from the sky on a full moon Thursday—what a festival!

DAAZ: I wander far along the path I dreamed of and get lost, now is the time to fly to Parnassus and rent some chairs; in the Garden of Eden, three owls walk without saying a single mU. Illuminate yourself, smile, and embrace the mystery of foreign affairs, invent an empire to dine and dance in *secula seculorum*... a spell? U-Ching is a Miracle!!

I dream up wild ideas, you blow planets, and the other... hugs lampposts. I have refined taste, I walk my path, I leap to the 8 and enter the underworld... I already know who I am, and there is no problem with that, I no longer know anything about anything... I love from the peak of a mountain, I see the immensity of the universe, now I make it into a verse... shall we speak of the Multiverse? U!!

Figs from another basket, sweet and fresh? Desert toads from Mexico and black beetles traveling guided by the Pleiades, are we getting lost?! U!!

Let's dance and breathe!! Hold me tight, for I only feel my heart, I gently inhale your donkey-skin scent without glasses, you have fallen into oblivion and comb your hair; yes, he occasionally speaks with a camel, says an old man who today is no one...

You see, we are all dressed up, gifted, embraced, like two fools!! *ApasiaU*, we kiss each other's mouths and ears, we look at ourselves in the mirror, and now—a rooster crows!! *UbÚ, King!!*

Up and down, give me a cricket, does a rabbit pass by?? Who said *crazy?* I illuminate myself, carallU, membrillU, carajillU, or pasillU!! Go with God, farewell, I leave with music to birth panthers, straight away, in a rocket, like a pirate losing my shoe!!

I am a drug you cannot control, forbidden fruit, don't even try it, I only want to play, love, and sing it out, with you!!

I'm at the *bare nostrum* making cod croquettes... and you?

If you want to fly, you must jump to the 8, from sun to sun, like an owl...

I walk alone, I catch everything on the fly, as if by chance... Now it rains, now the wind blows, and one day I will lose myself along these paths... deep inside, we are no fortune tellers, we decant wines and make windmills spin... let the violins play, and let the penguins enter!!

We set doves free, we climb the nine pines, we sing songs, we write rhymes, we make love, and we decant without measure, here we moan, and we cry!!

We are explorers of cyberspace, skidding and searching for love at dawn, only DadA knows where we're going—nothing separates us, and no one is waiting for us!!

Just dance, laugh, and hush!!

In the Marseille Tarot, a 7, a 9, and an 8 appear... are we already at infinity? Bastard!!

I raise my finger, crawl into bed, mesmerized, delirious, staring straight ahead... I make love to the night!!

What did you say? U!!

Acrobat, bastard, know-it-all, lunatic, and reckless gambler... What a game!!

Like when I was a kid—dirty, lost, loved, and wanted—who said that? Sharp!!

I wanted, I read, and I loved you all as best I could, I fell... I got up, and I cried out to the starry sky... black night!!

LOVE...

I searched and found you, I sang and dreamed, I imagined and lost... imagine, walk, and listen... yes, once again, the rebirth, the consciousness, the horizontal logarithmic elliptical spiral... wait and dance, holy patience!!

On the moon of Valencia, I dance it out with patience; I invent opaline, transalpine, crystalline concepts... deep within, here at night, we go all in... they call me *pixapins*, I wander the roads, all in the past, I climb to the rooftop, and look—a cat just passed by... now I eat an ice cream and make a mess of it all, like a lost little beetle!!

Brilliant, I'm lost, playing the gourmet, a little drunk, and on Sunday, I tip my hat!! Albert Hoffman? No, Ra Uru Hu!!

Beethoven's Ninth and Wittgenstein's Seventh... Kierkegaard didn't show up, he got lost, just like you, who no longer knows what to think; turn on the radar and learn to add; learn to sing... can you read?

What do you mean? Do you want to escape to another world? Look at you!!

Mysterious, we will lose ourselves... where space fades... cool from Paraguay, call me *julay*, call me *guey*, call me *carai*, *recoi*, or Uruguay!!

And JUPITER? Nobody knows, it's not in your mind, it's U, it's 4 U... It's only U!!

Dadarling... I don't mind, you see U?! My GOD!! Can't understand? This or that, I'm on my way... and U??

Madadamme: one more kissU!!

ChapeaU!!

Epilogue

I can't help but be realistic, but I will remain optimistic—it's just how my father taught me to see the world. I'm not lying when I say that Mariano had aristocratic manners or behaviors, yet he came from a rural background. He always carried himself like an untamed outsider, but make no mistake, he was a king. And I am a very particular kind of king—can you tell?

I don't hide it, and I often warn people: there are only three years left before a resounding end of an era! Don't think we come from a wealthy family—far from it. We have worked hard and struggled to understand cosmic and mystical matters, yet we've always remained rooted in Figueres and the vineyard. Among us, there are carpenters, architects, designers, and even a tailor. It would be foolish of me not to leave behind a legacy worthy of my beloved ancestors, wouldn't it? We are a peculiar family—beautiful people with a zest for life!

Of all the people I have known and loved, the one who truly held the reins was Grandma Dolors. She could just as easily read Kierkegaard as she could fry green peppers and serve carquinyolis with muscatel for dessert. I would read her some Dadaist treatise or one of my own poems, though, to be honest, with little success! Her eldest son, Mariano, also became a cook—and an architect at a very young age. By the time he was seven, he already knew. My father was a very particular kind of galactic being, and we all knew it. If he loved you, he protected you and gave you the very best—never less, he used to say. And I would tell him, "We are not of this world!"

The "Pacha" or the King has what he deserves because he takes care of his people. But one thing I can confess—and the facts speak for themselves—is that he educates those closest to him so that life may be eternal. My grandmother and my father embodied the figure of the Empress in the Tarot of Marseille, each ruling in their own way. But for me, the role of the Emperor falls into my hands—a number 4, ruled by Jupiter, opening sealed dimensions.

Since I am quite clear about my strengths and shortcomings, I have studied and met a few kings. The difference between them and me is that I *know*—and, in fact, I practice daily despite everything. With this book,

I wish for all of us to fare a little better. True synergy will lead us to a state of cosmic communion! Never stop trusting life—it teaches us, repeats lessons for us, and guides us where we need to go. With patience and kindness, everything becomes smoother and more understandable. After all, they say all roads lead to Rome! But remember, today, all empires fall.

At the same time, one must also understand that the world is very small. If you've made it this far, just know that one day, the seas will part before you—*only* if it is *you* who arrives, or *you* who leaves.

In truth, all you need to do is find your place to see what you are meant to see. Let your destiny be *yours* and not the one subtly imposed upon you.

Walk your path and be the best version of yourself. Breathe deeply, trust in who you already are—you are perfect, with all your "flaws," if only you recognize and nurture them! Be polite and have faith in your potential because the world needs you. The gods watch over you, love you, and guide you—never doubt it!

Regardless, you should know that very soon—or perhaps much sooner than expected—you will become an extraordinary case, unique and different… You will have what you have imagined or dreamed of. And if you have made it to the end, I leave you to meditate from *sun to sun,* all alone…

Do we know that we are on our way back home? Are we returning to the original source, where love expands??!!

My meditations and my desire for transcendence here on Earth make me think that we are already closer to one another, and that we must support each other, for life is long—and surely, sooner or later, we will meet again.

Like a movie about my own rebirth, the result of my solitary research, the journey you now hold in your hands has, so far, been well worth it. Through it, I have come to understand many things by seeking to challenge you and reach you. If I take on the role of the *Red King of Catalogne 3.0*, it is because I feel that it must be so—because I care for my own, and for those of you who voluntarily embark on this journey of conscious transformation and evolution. It seems that now is the time to grow!!

Protecting *sacred* knowledge means placing it in the right hands, sharing it, and making things easier in this rebirth—one that is both decadent, special, and magical. And in this story, *you* are the absolute protagonist, if you so choose. Yes, the river is life!!

Shall we celebrate?

Bon voyage!!

Leonardo Fibonacci

Lo Rei Roig 3.0 de la Catalonge
Agent 105 - Serp vermella magnèïica
Generador Manifestador emocional 1/3
Analista, consultor, confierenciant holístic
Poeta Dadaista humorista
Director del Clúster AvantGarden

leonardofibonacci45@gmail.com
Roc Pedrol Navarro / Facebook
leonardofibonacci45/ Instagram
www.drfrog45.com

What could be considered a prophecy, and also announces a resounding end, today is almost an evidence. Ra Uru Hu experienced a mystical encounter lasting eight days, during which a voice revealed to him how the universe works, how we are designed, and how to face this great mutation that is inevitably leading us to an evident end. *No choice, you are very lucky!! Jazz—be yourself!!*

Ra insisted that we have been *trained* to do things and to control, rather than to see and enjoy... Free yourself from your indoctrinated mind and learn to decide and see—while you still have time!!

From *Rat to Rat*, with infinite admiration: we will come to *be* and to *see* eternity... The quantum leap is evident, and we will witness the waters opening wide as we dance to unknown melodies!!

Mariano Pedrol Parunella, Arquitecte intergalàctic.
6/2 Generador Manifestant, Aquari. *Jazz be your self.*

Ra Uru Hu: Master of Masters, reincarnated **Socrates, 5/1 Ego Manifestor**, Cross of the Clarion.